SORRY,
BUT ... I'M
DIFFERENT

SHARIF NSUBUGA

ISBN: 9798394105975

DEDICATION

I love you, *mama.*

SORRY, BUT ... I'M DIFFERENT

Contents

CHAPTER ONE

I waited for a long time as life passed me by. Not that I don't live the challenges, I mean, we all do. Don't we? Being in America, the pandemic had just hit its core. And I promised myself to do anything, even if working in a fixed receptacle room consisting of a bowl with a flushing system.

It is not my home, but God bless America! I have spent fifteen years in San Francisco working myself out.

From the beginning, I had to fight for anyone to ever believe in me or even think I deserved…

I was born in Nigeria before I moved here in 2005 at eighteen years, no degree but a Secondary school certificate. I had done a lot of nothing for myself. A dark-skinned, broke-ass young man, working and living in one of the most luxurious cities as a retailer.

And growing up in Otodo-Gbame, one of the poorest and vulnerable areas in Lagos, my countrymen used to make comments about my skin complexion being yellowish. They would call me a yellow banana. I was so young then to realize what colorism meant.

Anyway, I stood close to a private fitting salon with frosted glass doors, awaiting a middle-aged woman who bought countless glamorous dresses. The tailors adjusted hems and embroiders added final flourishes while I sweet-talked her behind. She sipped on champagne, asking several questions while expecting me to respond accordingly.

"It's four thousand dollars, ma'am."

"More than your salary!" She made belittling remarks.

Back home, I used to feel different, and sometimes better.

Of course, I was dumb, and the colorism remarks had boosted my ego.

Not until I moved here, and it was my first time to realize what white people looked like. I remember in the train, sitting close to a not-young white man with blue eyes, and my dark skin brushed his---That reckoned my reality and I realized I was so black, even when they used to call me light-skinned. It felt like another universe, a place I didn't know I needed to accept myself.

My full symmetrical lips folded out of confusion, surely unable to respond due to this temporary shock caused by the offensive, impolite woman. She rolled up her hazel eyes as her tiny fingers picked up a mini black credit card, which she passed through the card machine at the wooden log.

Inside the house of H & Z, the atmosphere was perfumed with sandalwood scent, and the lighting was soft and tender, yet she reminded me of my skin complexion.

"What are you still doing here?" The ghostly manager raised his voice at me.

"What?" The corners of my mouth slightly frowned.

"Come on, Ahmed." He sweetened his tone when he noticed a chubby, dark-skinned woman's darting eyes on him, who had headed to the counter with several dresses as well. "Be a gentleman."

I stepped aside, my rugged fingers holding packs of glamorous dresses for the bitter customer as we passed my Korean brother with a dewless skin in a tailored navy suit who opened the door and we walked behind the discreet façade of brass to her parked black Mercedes-Benz.

While I placed them in the back of the car, she entered without a single word. This woman did not thank or tip me, and she drove off, disregarding my existence. Such experiences used to wear me down with crow's feet. Ha-ha. But at work, we never know who we will meet. Do we? It might be a canary with a fractured leg or a giant soulless rhino we have to put our hands up to its butt.

My parched forehead let go while these visual flashes of Chioma intoxicated my mind.

The woman yearned for.

Her almond-shaped eyes with depth mirrored my soul, and her fine coffee skin complexion. Also, her broad face with rounded-tipped nostrils showed our Yoruba ancestry. Her visuals made me feel safe and at home. But while I was immersed in my thoughts, a sudden, louder, sharp cough made by a no longer young man who stood close to his crumbling truck made me lose the pleasure as he continued clearing his throat.

His barks were dry, with a trembling hand as if he had a fever. In fact, my mature mind stopped working at the time, wondering what kind of creature made him sick; he struggled to breathe as his reddish brown eyes darted around like he needed help.

The gray-haired man momentarily lost his balance, and my quivering arm almost touched him before my rude manager shouted.

"He's sick." He made loud wails at the flanked entrance with sculptural planters.

"What?"

I got occupied with extreme uncontrollable fear, moisture excluded through the pores of my face, as I speedily took backward steps, far away from him. These were the bad days when the pandemic had wrecked the Western world.

"Seriously." The old man addressed the manager.

The poor, astonished old man had chest heaviness as I ran away from him.

I didn't want to lose my life!

No! At least, not then.

So many things I needed to do.

Besides, I had promised to see my

supernatural lady, Chioma, again. The only one who moved my frail wails. Not only that, but I gave my word for the greatest life when I returned to her. So, I always came to work acting like a pigeon, something that's nonthreatening to my white superiors.

And giving up was never an option for any nonwhite immigrant.

Right?

Back home, we used to hurt a lion to win over a girl's heart, and I never failed her, so in this torturous life, there was nothing compared to what we passed through.

"You! You're fired!" His wraithlike mouth thundered at the door.

The sudden, unexpected fact hit my face. Deep down, I always knew he wanted to fire me; however, he needed a perfect opportunity, and this may have been it. He was the owl in the daylight that my inner human heard but never saw coming until he snuffed my job away.

"What have I done?" I wondered.

"You're carelessly out of the counter without a mask on… And besides, you're having encounters with sick people! See." He looked for many excuses not to sound like an owl, but I definitely knew what he meant, and I surely respected his decision

"But you asked me to assist…" I tried to give him a proper explanation, but he interrupted.

"See, buddy… I don't want to listen to your F excuses!" He bit his rounded jaws, and I squirmed in my skin.

"Please."

"My decision is final. Get the fuck out of this place." His cracked arms slammed the door.

"Fine!"

CHAPTER TWO

January 31ˢᵗ, 2020

The reddish sun rose across the sky, casting golden shadows through my torn curtain bedroom window, with a dusty yellowish-brown color. Also, the cracks in the roof filtered some dawn air and damp earth scent, even though I didn't bother to get up.

Perhaps I didn't have the strength to face the truth; I had become a jobless man in a foreign land. This portrayed a weak man back home; we were supposed to be out there, hunting for our families.

It showed a very responsible man. Besides, I had passed the age of marrying, thirty-three years had passed, and the pressure was so high. The way I was raised at home, my mama always taught me to become a husband, and Chioma gave me a glimpse of hope for fulfilling my duties as a man.

'WHERE IS YOUR WIFE?' had become the question ever since I finished my Secondary school, since the Mosque did not allow sex before marriage, so she worried about what would happen in case I got a girl pregnant. She had me at seventeen years, and maybe this played a role in her anxiety.

And also a nonverbal rule in our culture, as a man by thirty, you must've a wife or else your manhood will be socially scrutinized and questioned. It's a strict rule, even though sometimes she said, 'I would rather you live your life and go towards your career.' But still she teased like 'Ṣé o ní ọ̀rẹ́bìnrin kan báyìí?'

'Do you currently have a girlfriend?'

However, no one could hire me anyway, not this time of the pandemic when President Donald Trump had ordered quarantine for all one hundred ninety-five U.S citizens who were repatriated back from Wuhan, China.

I rubbed my brown nut eyes and held on to my wide, hairy arms with a yawn. Then I folded the creamy, frayed bed on the cold, uneven floor, with a rusty blanket and a lumpy pillow. A monstrous rodent, a king-sized mouse, speedily came out of the hole in the black couch into the narrow, filthy toilet with a jerry can of water beside a blue basin.

I can't go back home. No! I haven't accomplished what I promised my beautiful Chioma. A fancy safe home in Abuja, and a comfortable life she truly deserved. As a man who lives abroad, they expected me to go beyond their imaginations. Yet no one in their mind would ever imagine I slept in bugs to survive and also sustain them, sticking and sucking my whole body.

I heard sudden louder knocks on the brown wooden door while my brows pulled. I stood on my wide bare feet without the sandals, and my rugged arm opened up the door.

A chubby middle-aged woman with a drawn, tight face expelled air from her lungs in a deliberate manner while her blue eyes squinted against the force of a sharp cough she eventually made up front. Neither did I pull or lean away. And a pool of sweat streamed across her forehead.

My eyes widened while I shrank inside, closing the door and expelling air from my lungs heavily with simultaneous tears; these were the insufferable days. I ran to my atrocious toilet, covering my broad, bridged nose, and picked up the white bar of soap tied to the window grill. My chocolate fingers washed my nose properly with clean water from the rusty tap of the sink while a faint dust and last night's stew invaded me.

"Shit!"

She kept on banging on my patched plywood door heavily. I paced around with my tapping feet since I didn't know what to do. In the process, I speedily grabbed my long black bag stained with cobwebs and time, then picked up my savings under the rusting cling to the pillow stuffed with my old clothes, which I definitely placed into my pockets.

I'd been trying to have the balls to return home forever, and maybe she was the sign. Inside my wails, I heard a calling out there that I needed a change. For years, I had been arching for people I love, working from morning to evening, but I had never discovered myself. How about my happiness? Life is a complicated, dangerous game that tests how far we can go for the people we love by pushing us further than we can sustain.

I placed on my blue mask and a black jacket with a shabby quality as I took a few steps toward the door. I had unsettling breath in my narrow bones since the uninvited guest became quiet all of a sudden. How much further can I really go for the people I love? Rang in my mind, and I took a shallow breath while I opened; whatever life planned to throw at me, unfortunately, the woman coldly lay on the floor. Her sharp nose was reddish brown, and white substances came out of her ghostly, dry mouth onto the concrete.

Maybe for once I needed to be brave enough before I became short, and I had one more shot at a lifetime. In life, we always have a shot to hit the jackpot, and to me, it was Chioma. I was willing to give her everything I got, even if risking my life to see her for the last time.

I bent myself up immediately after my soaking wet eyes landed on this stranger's no longer alive body. The strap was on, and the pandemic had made a final check at my door. At the moment I had to decide if I was willing to die in my thin bed or go and have last experiences for a lifetime. My shallow boots stretched past her as I ran out of my apartment without thinking where to go, down to the street in the Mission District.

I did not want to close my eyes while life passed me by again.

I would've regretted...

Inside the house of H & Z, the golden lights cascaded from the broad Chandeliers as a spectral manager noticed a brown young boy picking up a pack of black undies. His reddish eyes lay on him throughout as he placed his black phone on the wooden log.

This boy, dressed in black shorts and a red hoodie, dropped the pack into his pocket while his eyes darted around to make sure no one noticed. His tiny fingers then kept on touching a number of garments in the same row, close to the velvet armchairs in deep emerald. Not only that, but a not-young woman passed with a working employee in a navy blue suit to the minimalist mannequins displaying the dresses she may have yearned for.

The manager's wide, phantasmic face had a cocky grin as he slowly moved to the exit. His dry mouth swallowed up a thick gravel as he waited for him. The poor boy reached the frosted door where he seized him.

"Got you! You spoiled brat."

He exerted a lot of energy on his tense, rounded neck, strangling him.

The boy's feet were still struggling to get free from the restraint, but his phantasmal, rugged arm had so much energy. The boy's arm began trembling like an earthquake as he weakened further, struggling to breathe. His half-closed eyes sheened a forced cough onto his brown mutton-chopped beard.

"Fuck!" He exclaimed.

With less fog clearing the pale blue skies, I walked toward a Chinese-style roasted crab restaurant on a tree-lined street. The air was sharp but not cruel. Besides, their coffee area was not so far away from my apartment, and my brownish eyes looked at the two overdressed ladies in short skirts who sat close to the window, winking at me as I made an order. Suddenly, the shop's television got turned on, and there was breaking news on the screen.

"Hey! Please increase the volume." I

requested.

A youthful brunette lady wearing a denim apron looked at me while handing the television remote into my rugged palms. Without turning, I increased the volume, even when I could still hear the click of mugs inside the restaurant. The décor was warm but unsophisticated, just enough within the brick walls and reclaimed wooden tables that had a soft glow from the narrow displayed lights hanging on the ceiling.

"Breaking news, fifty-two residents around the Bay Area are confirmed dead. The State Mayor, London Breed, is going to address her state in a few minutes." I had a sudden force in my throat as if I needed to vomit at the fact that another chubby woman lay dead in front of my apartment entry.

"Ha-ha! Do you believe that?" Her curved lips ratio of 1:2 opened.

I turned my angular jaw toward hers, speechless, while giving her an awkward smile. I was never used to being visible around people like her. At least not since then.

Not only that, but she ran her pole-like arm,

tousling her hair and giving me a quick handshake with her tender palm still stained with coffee spills.

"I'm Jacqueline." She introduced herself.

"I'm Ahmed…" I cleared my throat while I rubbed the back of my neck, "Ahmed Olaoluwatomijogun."

My boots crisscrossed slightly beneath the table as I took some time to respond.

"What? OLAULA…" She raised her brows to her temples. "What does your name mean?'

With her tucked, wiggling arms on the table, I realized how young she could be, maybe around mid-twenties, and I pulled away.

"The wealth of God is enough inheritance for me."

"Well, sounds like a nice name, Ahmed." She gave me a cup of thick black coffee with an unavoidable, contagious smile, which slightly made me very uncomfortable.

CHAPTER THREE

February 1st, 2020

Before I migrated from Nigeria, my single mama always nurtured me with hard work and discipline. She did the relentless work on her own and exemplified those values in me, no matter the obstacles or challenges in life. Also, my education was always a top priority since she never finished hers. My late grandparents had her drop out since they needed to control the narrative before our tribe realized her balloon-like belly.

Mr. Olaoluwatomijogun, my late grandfather, cursed that day he allowed her to go to school. Women used to be taught to become housewives and value marriage only, which was sad, and the pressure was so high when they were permitted to go to school, since false narratives about educated women ran around like the wind.

The tender air, tinged with a sandalwood scent, hit my nose as the golden rays fully entered the room, with its ornate, crown-molded ceilings. My hands ran through my eyes, emerging from a deep sleep. My long, structured arms stretched out, exposing my hairy armpits while I strangely gazed around the entire place.

I couldn't access the previous events that may have led me to this beautiful studio apartment. The gigantic white bed, low to the ground, close to the white cotton carpet, the pillows scattered like pollen in the air, two with strands of hair opposite the medium black shelf with blue organized jeans, close to a massive closet.

"Look, who's awake?" Jacqueline said as she walked into the white elephantine room. Her white palms carried a ceramic plate of beans, eggs, toasted bread, and a glass of juice in bed. My nut eyes were widely stuck on her; she had on my long, pale black t-shirt, exposing her thick, well-proportioned thighs, and I slightly leaned away.

Sexual intercourse and marriage are seen as a prestige and privilege in my culture, so I panicked. More like an elevation status. Back home, we are not even supposed to be close to any woman we have not yet paid a bride price for. As a man without a wife in Nigeria, I always sensed the treatment difference, and also respect.

My throat swallowed my doubts as I placed on a smile to appreciate her.

"Thank you!"

"It's nothing."

Her hazel eyes met mine, and I lost the seconds I took watching her like a plague of diamonds.

"You have to eat." Her cheeks had tiny, rounded dimples as she shimmered like a sun.

I placed a silver fork in the cooked beans while staring at her again, but clearly, she noticed my quivering arm and tensed angular jaws.

"Is something wrong?" She pulled her well-knitted eyebrows. "Oh, you don't like the meal? I can cook something else for you."

"Come on, you drugged me… And now you want to drug me more." I came to the obvious conclusion while folding my squared forehead.

"No… I haven't."

She ran her arm behind her small ear with no eye contact.

"I don't believe you."

"All right…" She stood up, walking around the cotton carpet. "I… I did."

How was I supposed to protect myself from her? My full, textured lips opened as I placed the ceramic plate aside.

"I didn't mean to. I just didn't want to be alone." She shuffled her little, pretty feet while rubbing her rounded neck.

"This whole place became bigger for me… especially in this pandemic."

Her reasoning was so young, and my arm pulled up my black trousers close to the one wall with a textured wallpaper of a woven pattern. I had gotten used to these owls taking things from him without consent. At home, I would've been conditioned to marry her since in my culture, you must marry the woman you have intercourse with, but here it was a woman's world. If it made her happy, who am I to have said otherwise?

"Please." I requested my t-shirt, and she took these slow steps close to me, her height was around five feet three inches, as her arms undressed, exposing her daggling, well-defined breasts. My darting eyes looked away as I froze. She handed the shirt, and I placed it on quickly while holding up my not-clean black bag on a woven rug in front of the door.

"Please," Jacqueline begged me.

I had lost trust in her, especially since her actions and words were different things.

"I tried, ma'am. I tried." My chocolate fingers opened the door, and I walked out of her apartment.

Throughout my whole life here, people looked at me and thought I was a hard guy, probably a little mean or tough, without knowing me, yet I had to learn the hard way to never soften around white girls, especially in their suburban neighborhoods. I've had a very humble beginning. I used to be that black kid who ran carefree on the streets of Otodo-Gbame, but in America, I became the over-policed man questioned for even breathing.

I had to work hard to sustain myself... I was dead sure they paid me the least at my last job. Inside the luxurious house of H & Z, the shadowy manager began coughing behind the counter as the middle-aged Korean woman in a blue navy suit worked on an Italian man. Her brown hand had lined several archival sketches while she looked back at his glassy eyes in search of breath.

Immediately she finished with the elderly customer, she turned with a lot of curiosity.

"What?" His dry, cracked lips produced a hoarse tone.

"Come on, Phillip." She smoothened her voice.

"We're more than friends. You can tell me anything." While tucking her curtain bang hair behind her medium-sized ear.

"Haven't you learnt proper English yet?" He pulled his brows in the middle of his nose. "I SAID it's just a simple cough. Nothing serious to worry about."

"You sure?' She insisted.

His not-smooth chubby cheeks seemed flushed from exertion, appearing like botched patches of colorlessness, and his nose became reddish brown as moisture exuded through the pores of his skin. He then began making louder, sharper coughs.

"Yes! Now get back to work." He insisted.

She hesitated to turn to the counter, but she did, anyway, working on the woman with a child. However, her abrupt arm movements called the muscular security guard who stood at the frosted exit door while she wrote a note secretly and handed it to him.

The brown brother walked away with tightened jaws immediately he read the note saying, "We need to take him out." His brownish eyes met Phillip's as if they asked who was going to strike first.

The recent events had me thinking about Chioma, when we were in Secondary school, and also the last time I saw her. I had just gotten a B1 visa, which my traveling agent claimed to be changeable to a student visa once I reached the States. My mama and I sold the only seven acres of land we had for this opportunity, and it turned out to be a scam. I, as a man, had to run with a lie; I could never have broken my mama's heart, nor seen the whites in her chocolate eyes.

No, she had been through enough...

And I was so angry, sad, and a depressed person since I took the difficult decision to stay away from the people I love. I used to be so close… very close---to my mama, and while I struggled to get things better at home, she got really sick… I would've moved back if I knew how serious it was. She started getting worse and worse, and she passed away on September 21st, 2010.

It was a Tuesday, but not a mere Tuesday… One minute past mid-day… I still recall everything. And I will carry that baggage of guilt on my shoulders wherever I am, for how I failed to protect her like any other man she had in life. The chest heaviness and red-blue flamed sensations are excruciating. That pain peeled off my frail walls, leaving me vulnerable and motherless, but it still brings some joy the times I see the flashes of her cocoa-skinned face. Man, my mama was such a good person. She was. Ms. Abimbola just happened to have met life in the most atrocious way.

I made up my mind to go back home; life had become too short to be wasted. At first, I had this quick fear of losing her if I didn't meet what I promised, but when I watched Mayor

London Breed's speech on quarantine, I realized I might die in this foreign land, without taking at least a last glance at my beautiful African woman.

Life isn't always about financial stability or wealth, as I used to think, but love. And those small moments we live with the people we adore are priceless. They're more than anything in the world, and I could trade anything to see my mama again.

ANYTHING! But now… I couldn't.

I picked up my mobile phone and visited the Brussels Airlines website. My face twisted with lines of confusion immediately I noticed the statement saying, "Flights closed up right now."

I hopelessly scrolled down the webpage, and unexpectedly, I saw a Brussels flight leaving in two hours. The corners of my lips clicked as I smiled, taking a quick cab to the airport.

The house of H & Z that once whispered luxury became a faded rug, the loud call made by the brown woman when an ambulance parked at the façade smoked glass, rang like an alarm bell, and five doctors covered in white

Tyvek suits walked inside. The Korean woman in a blue mask at the counter pointed at Phillip, the ill-mannered manager.

"What have you done?"

His pale arms stilled, trembling on the counter.

"Please, Sir, it's just a simple cough!"

He addressed one of the doctors in an N95 mask as he stood from his cushioned seat.

The doctors grasped him since he resisted, giving a diazepam injection, and they put him in a Tyvek suit, and an N95 mask sealed tightly, covering his medium reddish eyes and dry, cracked mouth.

Not only that, but a doctor with slivery-white hair approached the Korean woman.

"What's your name?" Her gloved hands held a sheet and a black pen for recordings.

"Eleanor Ha-yoon."

"I am Doctor Sarah." She looked at the Murano Chandeliers that gave a soft glow to the store.

"Did anyone else get in physical contact with him?"

"Well, I am not sure, but I think so because

he is our manager."

"Are all the workers around?" She turned her average body with tensed jaws.

"Not all of us. Some work certain shifts, and also different days and nights."

"All right. Do you have all their addresses and contacts?" She continued.

"Yes."

Inside the terminal with surging suitcases, voices ringing like bees, and sharp, short announcements made, I speedily reached the desk clutching my boarding pass. My brown boots stood still at the Brussels check-in reception. The two little kids with Barbie dolls sprawled across two seats, and a man seated close by with a Bluetooth earpiece.

"Please, Sir, I'm requesting, I need to be on that leaving flight."

I begged the gypsum-toned man in a tailored charcoal blazer.

"No… It's full."

His impeccable posture did not change as he declined my request on the spot.

I walked around as my sculpted arms dropped. Also, my nut eyes became watery, but

I never planned to give up, as I always did. There was more to live for, out there, and I was willing to do anything, so I turned to the Brussels staff once again.

"I beg you, brother… I need to be on that flight."

"And I said it's full---Full... I don't know what language you want me to use, but you're on standby." The man gave me the same attitude they have always given me, anyway, like he never mattered.

"Onye isi, why are you rude? Is it my accent or color?" I thundered my voice and drew everyone's eye, crying for help, even when I knew I was voiceless.

"I wasn't---All right… You will be on the flight." He made low whispers.

CHAPTER FOUR

I had made awesome connections with my coworkers, apart from the manager. He never liked me; maybe I gave him a bitter taste in his mouth. For fifteen years, I had never once received any good vibes from the man, to my delight and surprise, actually. Dude, I didn't even know you lost your wife and two boys in a hit-and-run accident, and it wrecked my soul when Eleanor slipped her pinkish tongue during our lunch break. While the natural light shone through the curved benches in the façade, there was grass where the lined trees that stood behind the house of H & Z.

I had always seen your dislocated shoulder, but she revealed the scar came from being diagnosed with leukemia at the age of thirteen years. And you went through five years of chemotherapy... Phillip, I had no idea, and your story wrecked my soul.

Maybe I even moved back home because of you. We humans tend to devalue what is in front of us and dream of another world. We forget that we still have life, the most precious gift of all, more valuable than anything we think we need. And there is someone on that hospital bed, especially this time, longing to get better and live an adventure again.

The fluorescent lights dimmed overhead, spilling sideways through the gap beneath the door, splintered and paled, casting long shadows to Eleanor's rounded face, with pale and flawless skin, who had let her edges touch the well-built security man's bowlike lips. His craggy, sweaty fingers squashed her flat booty while they kissed like Romeo and Juliet.

Her baby's eyes closed, and he moved his bumpy fingers in unparalleled positions of her inwards while their kiss was tender like they tasted red wine for a few seconds, it deepened, nose to nose as their breath raised, and left hands connected in her sea burrow.

She got turned on by his circular movements inwards, her brown, tiny fingers tightly held onto the toilet's white stalls as she let him take control of her entire body.

From nowhere, they heard a knock on the door. Eleanor's eyes widened, and she pulled out his uneven fingers.

"Eleanor!" A weighty voice called from the outside.

"Shit!" She whispered while rubbing her fingers on her mouth.

"Hello!"

"Just give me a minute!" Eleanor's darting eyes rolled.

His words shattered their hush. She passed a wet wipe on her small face, covering it with a blue mask, and then opened the wooden door lightly.

"Doctor Sarah wants you."

The dark-skinned security guard in a navy suit addressed her.

"Oh, Jasper."

Eleanor exclaimed while she held his chocolate fingers to walk away, but Jasper's brown eyes had already seen a man's shadow in the stall. His narrow forehead had parched as they moved towards the green hedges that headed to the front of the store.

Two men in Tyvek suits stood in the entrance with their alert eyes scanning for inconsistencies, as Eleanor reached the parked black Mercedes-Benz. This woman with sliver-white hair puffed on her burning cigarette, clearly occupied by countless visual flashes. Her well-knitted brows furrowed, not in confusion, but in empathy. She pulled out her Lithobid capsule and took it with a bottle of water before her hazel eyes landed on the stranded Eleanor from far.

"What's with that?"

"It lessens my anxiety." As she approached her. "Such a busy year!"

Her lean shoulders sloped forward, not from tiredness but perhaps from several deaths she may have witnessed.

"We need contacts for the missing workers and their addresses."

Doctor Sarah parched her forehead with dotted freckles.

"Let me print it out."

"Okay."

The terminal organized hums were mixed with a variegated pattern of languages and small suitcases. Also, these ongoing notices echoed overhead in English, Dutch, and French. A not-young man, around fifty-eight years old, with a coffee skin, shattered in pidgin French while he took a bite of his dark smoked maize, and I stood in the long, uneven line among countless people of color.

A tall, tiny woman, dressed in a charcoal blazer, smiled at every passenger who passed through the immigration office.

This white boy in the hoodie scrolled through his phone, and his fingers trembled slightly. His chubby Indian neighbor had his arms in the pockets; shivering, he surely might've been nervous to reach the officer behind the glass. However, everyone had gotten scared, and we all believed in our inauspicious ending. It seemed like a life and death situation, and don't get me wrong, we saw several deaths. My rugged fingers scrubbed my heavy, black sheepish hair in the process.

It was a difficult yet essential situation to survive for the people we love, so many people depended on us. My goodness, this period was brutal, and everyone outlasted through the reliance on people and family. But immediately, you lose them, you lose yourself.

I stepped forward, and this youthful officer

with brown eyebrows didn't greet me but asked for my passport.

"Where are you going?"

"Lagos, Naija."

"Purpose?"

"I'm going home!"

I pulled my mask off my face for a few seconds, and he scanned my passport, and his white fingers tapped the keyboard. I had a sudden shortage of breath. Not only that, but I could sense the eyes on my back of an elderly woman with a scarf who coughed.

I was given an exit from the United States, and I walked past the checkpoint into the duty-free zone. Bags and accessory ads flashed on digital screens. Also, I saw a few people sipping on wine in different bars while I searched for my gate---GT33. I reached the Brussels aircraft door as my phone began ringing, and a man in a tailored suit directed me to my seat. I checked it out, and an unknown number got displayed.

My chocolate face bent with parallel lines as I switched off my phone and entered the tremendous airplane.

A well-proportionate gentleman welcomed me on board immediately I walked in slowly, looking around for my seat. His coat was labelled with his name, Le Floris, and I took my seat while expelling air from my lungs heavily. Other passengers kept moving slowly behind.

My heart died of uncontrollable joy. I had prayed for a time like this. Not with the pandemic, but when I moved back home and fulfilled my duties as a man. My eyes squinted with a crow's feet at the corners while I smiled. I wished Mama lived to see what she made of me. I couldn't believe it. I had lost hope of ever returning home, and this journey meant the world. I missed EGUSI soup and POUNDO yams; also, these salivating, vivid images of my delicate Chioma blurred my brown eyes.

I preferred marrying a woman from Nigeria because we come from the same tribe and background. Also, we were raised the same, so I wouldn't need to over-explain my culture on why I did, ate, or dressed a certain way. Not only that, but her deep, dark chocolate complexion was a masterpiece of nature, with her high cheekbones that sculpted her fine face.

'She's a goddess!'

The enormous plane smelled like recycled rubber air while I raised my brows high immediately I saw this wild brunette lady sitting opposite me near a narrow corridor where Le Floris greeted me again, but I had frozen in my seat, wondering what else she needed from him.

In the Mission District, the only filtering light came from the golden and pinkish late sunset rays that hit the ancient building near a cheap pub. The air hung heavy as a five feet ten inches tall man in a navy blue attire came out of the police car, and he entered a Chinese-style roasted crab restaurant. His clean-shaved face covered with a white mask as he walked straight to the pub's wooden counter, where he found an elderly man with a goat's beard serving three drunk men.

"Hello!"

"Hey, officer. We have good spirits here."

The old man's arm touched the table.

"Do you know him?"

The policeman's tone became a little serious

while he handed him a certain photo.

CHAPTER FIVE

My inner human sensed that I could never have proved myself innocent, and also, I had been exploited my whole life in the States. Everything my traveling agent said was a lie, and I lost so much trust in their system, not only that, but also my mama's life.

Honestly, nothing can ever justify why I never called the police, and I put one hundred percent blame on myself. I've always looked at the worst scenarios in life, which can be a draining and unhealthy way. I was very nervous about what might happen when they found that white woman in the entry of my apartment door, and I had this force in my dry throat of wanting to throw up whenever I recalled the event.

The once lived in room with uneven concrete floors, scattered sandals, and a blue basin had a five feet three inches tall man freeze in one position. It was dim, and his boots stood close to the door entry with his eumelanin complexion. This sulfur odor, like cabbage, invaded his broad, defined nostrils while his chocolate eyes landed on these green and blue bottle flies that were feeding and also laying eggs all over the rounded face of the unrecognizable dead woman who lay in front of my apartment.

His full, curved lips opened, he almost ejected matter from his black mini potbelly, and he deeply expelled air from his lungs due to the nasty, sickening odor that came out of the middle-aged woman. The houseflies swarm around the plywood door to lumpy stuffed pillows and also through the torn curtain as he loosened his tie and sagging the knot. His phone rang, and he received the call with his sloped shoulders.

"There is a dead body on the floor."

"Really!"

A metallic feminine voice echoed, and he tensed his chiseled jaws.

"Yes."

His brownish eyes became soaking wet.

"All right---Justin. It's okay, we're on the way there." She assured him.

The polished dove grey marble floors shimmered the soles of Eleanor, who had a cinnamon-scented spray, and antiseptic liquids she used to clean them in different rows until they gleamed like milk. The measures had been taken so they could open the House of H & Z soon.

From nowhere, her small pale face drawn tight, squinting her brown eyes from the force of the cough. She looked around as her arms positioned the two mannequins, placing them back in their respective rows. As she continued, her eyes landed on Jasper. The security boy in a navy suit had several fresh fibrous tissues on his baby's coffee face. Her fingers uncontrollably dropped the scummy cloth on the marbles.

"Jasper! What happened?"

Her rounded forehead was parched with curled lines. She had always taken care of him, especially in the foster homes where they lived together. Following his eating history, he was never a meat-eater, so she cooked vegan foods for him. Eleanor made a conscious decision on their behalf since she was almost thirty on September 4th, 2020, and he was only twenty-two. As someone who loved animals, Jasper never consumed them, yet their foster parents only cooked meat-related products.

He would never have been able to sustain himself without her; she was his North Pole that strengthened him. Jasper is really a sweet boy, and I never had any issues with him. He was so young when I first saw him, and bubbly, excited about a lot of things. Like, I didn't remember when I last felt like a bird in the States.

"Come on, little bro. You know you can tell anything."

Anyway, Eleanor's plumpy fingers touched his bruised, chubby cheeks. While he made not-so-loud wails with his streaming eyes, she ended up hugging him.

"Who did this to you?" She opened her textured lips as the middle-aged woman passed by, with four adorable children.

The skies had turned inky black with shimmering marks around a high-security disease research laboratory carved into the ground like a chronic wound, undergoing non-healing resolutions. It was a lackluster, greyish building with low reinforced concrete walls and sealed windows. Not only that, but with this crispy scent of the wet soil and faint rust of the perimeter fence having electricity.

A six-foot-one-inch-tall man with a blend of dark, white, and gray hair dressed in a lifeless white coat and unlaced boots smashed his short, burning cigarette, and he approached Doctor Sarah. Her flat booty had settled inside the black Mercedes-Benz driver's seat as she expelled carbon in the air. Her silvery-white hair was tucked into a surgical cap.

"You must be kidding me!"

He opened his cracked lips, drawing her eye.

"What?" Her hazel eyes darted around.

"The samples came from stalls, drains, cages, and carts used to transport animals."

His pale brows pulled together while he raised his raspy voice.

"It might be some sick shit going on."

"What do you mean?" Her gloved hands threw the burning cigarette; maybe she couldn't stand his manly attitude.

"It looks like Raccoon dogs' DNA or maybe civet cats."

"Doctor Colton? What exactly do you

mean?"

"We believe these animals were sold live at their market."

She leaned away, closing up the gull-winged door, and Doctor Colton stood firmly as she drove away, leaving him startled. His statement seemed like a blessing or a curse, but regardless of what, he was still stuck with her and needed to adapt or strengthen their working relationship. It was the only way we all survived this period anyway.

The light dimmed to a soft amber, and trolleys rolled out as the man in a suit leaned close to my sheepish hair. "Chicken or vegetarian?" while my Indian neighbor, who sat in the middle, watched a Bollywood film, and his brown, bearded face shimmered with flickering scenes.

"Chicken, please."

"Do you want a drink, sir?"

"Yes, please."

"All right, water or juice!"

"Water."

He handed a compact tray with rice, chicken sauce, a rolled plastic square of chocolate, and a bottle of water, and he quickly moved to the next passenger, behind me. A youthful couple across my seat whispered and giggled, their arms brushing over one another. While this brunette lady exchanged seats with my Indian neighbor.

Jacqueline and I were so different in many ways, but maybe being different could work in today's world. I had a sickening intuition, every time I looked into her hazel eyes with a sunburst effect around the pupil, and a gradient green on the outer Iris. I could read that she trusted me. Maybe I was supposed to be her meat shield, and she was mine.

My ride or die, baby.

"Man, what do you want from me?"

I crisscrossed my arms on my bursting pectorals as she took a seat next to me. Not only that, but my nut eyes watched her slightly like a glimpse of flash. She exposed her pearly teeth while her light cotton hand tucked her strands behind her small ear.

"Nothing." She softened her high-pitched voice.

I had never dated any woman from the

States, because there's a difference. I tried seeing this one curved girl who was Nigerian but born in America when mama used to be in my business, pressuring me to marry. However, I feel like the spark never sipped all the way, maybe the physical and sexual attraction. I feel like I wouldn't consider her Nigerian since she still had the African-American culture more than the Nigerian culture.

I slightly frowned, my textured lips with a wrinkled nose.

"Not again, UGHA."

"I'm not lying," Jacqueline leaned in, reducing the space between us.

"No, no, no… I am done with your UGHA, lies."

A sudden, complete absence of sound occupied the atmosphere as Jacqueline leaned away with a shut mouth.

"I… I think you should go back to your seat."

My wet side eye wandered as she picked herself up from my neighbor's seat, and I had a massive heartache. Maybe I went a little hard on her, but I needed to protect myself. I pushed my right foot behind the other to give her enough space to leave.

In the dusty hallway with flies, two examiners in Tyvek suits carried the woman's body in a faded cotton nightgown, tied like a finger in an ambulance as Doctor Sarah made immediate calls. Her eyes flicked between the body and the clipboard she held.

Not only that, but several people holding manmade billboards lingered, their arms across their chests around the perimeter tapes. These protesters scattered in a severe wave with their eyes wide open while several policemen blocked them from getting into the epidemic zone.

Doctor Sarah's eyes landed on the two billboards showing thousands of cases in the Mission District. The other said, 'You only protect and serve the white supremacists.'

She speedily asked her doctors to evacuate the premises. The world had turned upside down; these people were desperate and needed answers for the deaths of their loved ones.

Behind her, Justin, the black police officer,

stood firmly with an African American woman in a light khaki shirt and darker brown trousers, around forty-five years old, who hugged him.

"She was so pale!" His hand had covered his soaking wet eyes.

"You didn't know, this isn't your fault… All right." The sheriff comforted him.

"I should have come earlier, maybe I would have…"

"No…. Please don't do this to yourself."

She held onto his angular jaws with strong eye contact.

"I am scared." He frowned, his curved lips as colorless liquid rolled down to his rounded neck.

"It's okay to be scared, it's really okay."

CHAPTER SIX

February 2nd, 2020

The white walls had been stripped with no posters or family photos, just pale like a dry pheomelanin skin of someone long unwell. The fluorescent lights cast a desert gleam that flattened some sections covered with a transparent plastic sheeting, taped down, and with foaming temporary barriers.

Many patients lie still, experiencing difficulties in expelling air from their lungs properly. Not only that, but the atmosphere was heavy with alcohol fumes from overworked ventilators.

A brown lady, one of the one hundred ninety-five people from Wuhan, China, lay on one of the row beds that stood like an island opposite Phillip's bed space. She was in a critical, undesirable condition since the monitors flashed with abnormal oxygen saturation below ninety-five percent, and her treatment surely cost a lot; she could barely breathe in the tubing snaked from the IV poles to their arms, from the oxygen tanks to their dry, cracked faces.

"I can't feel my forehead, lord, the pain is going to split my head off." She cried.

"If it makes you feel better, I've never peed standing up until I was twenty-five."

A young lady, trained in the care of sick patients, pathetically seemed not to be experienced enough for such a complex structure. Maybe because their last nurse had just passed away. But before he died, the man with grey sheepish hair told them to never lose hope or belief in getting better, no matter what. He was one of the first care workers to die of COVID in the United States, coming from Miami. Phillip and the elderly Chinese woman seemed not to have yet processed his passing.

Guess now we share a mutual feeling since I have never gotten over my mama's death either.

Maybe I craved for closure, no wonder I decided to take this journey back home. I still wore this little bracelet where I etched her rounded chocolate face on the right side, full of soul.

She was full of soul…

Losing my mama was a huge slap in my face, and the itchy arch isn't describable enough. It deepened with time like an unclosed wound, and we hold onto our breath so we may never lose the little pieces and memories we shared. Or forget about their voices and what they actually smelled like. It's been more than ten years now that I have been playing the role of a strong African man who keeps it all together.

Like a Yoruba man who doesn't shed a tear because society would be so harsh if I ever expressed my emotions. Like, how dare I show my weakness as a man? But I was so sad and angry at myself. Oh, I was so heartbroken, and I am still.

Anyway, their new nurse had covered her face with an N95 mask and also sealed herself in a Tyvek suit while she attended to his neighbor as he tried to crack a joke.

Weak Phillip observed the wide human fragility room, having several patients in pain, but as time continued, his eyes blurred, and his lashes drooped. He shook his lean body like an earthquake while the Persian nurse speedily turned him, face down, to help his lungs expand as the machines made louder noises as if he was in a state of letting go.

She pressed her gloved palms onto his hairy chest while his back rose and fell for a while like floods that barely kiss the shore. His oxygen saturation was eighty-nine, so low as the nurse adjusted his mask and tightened the straps. In a few seconds, he came forth, his wrinkled nose expelled a lot of air from his lungs heavily, as his face began to flush.

In the long rectangular train, stood Eleanor's security lover, deeply occupied with intimate flashes they had. His eyes had become glassy and unfocused, scanning the dark outside empty playgrounds. Also, every other seat was blocked off with caution tape. From nowhere, his black eyebrows knitted with a force of cough, and he began barking while holding on to the plastic passenger stand for support.

The hum of the Brussels plane's engine deepened as the air became cool, mixed with the lifeless coffee scent from the cabin wipes, which a slim stewardess picked up alongside the used plastic cups and plates slowly, but as she held up the first five rows' garbage, she noticed the medium-sized Indian man coughing. Her heart raced over a hundred thirty beats, and a sudden uncontrollable fear of anxiety preoccupied her.

"Mr.?" She approached him.

"Mr. Advik,"

He shivered, shaking his headphones close to the Congolese man who dozed off with a pale scarf on his eumelanin face.

"Are you feeling well, sir?"

She tensed her sharp jawline while we experienced small turbulences that made me check my fastened seatbelt.

"No… I mean, yeah… I am having a little flu." He stammered.

The skies were a blend of violent flames and copper streaks as the aircraft began to descend. In the control room, having numerous screens flickering with satellite feeds, radar sweeps, and live footage from the airport perimeter, the elderly pilot received a radio call from the station. His younger copilot, dressed in a white shirt, dark navy blue blazer, and a black tie, picked up without hesitation.

"Flight SN 501, this is Zaventem Control."

"Yes, you're talking to the copilot of Captain Clinton Verhaegen."

"We communicated that there should be no passengers on board; Belgium is under a restrictive regulation." His deeper raspy voice produced a serious tone.

"Yes, we informed the States, but they insisted, and also requested a consideration of the Belgian passengers on board." Pilot Clinton grasped the radio call from him.

"Do not proceed with landing. I repeat, do not proceed with landing." The air became intense. "Hold at twelve thousand feet as we handle the situation on the ground."

Not only that, but they heard a flight attendant's call on the door, Clinton's copilot pressed a tight button to open, and the narrower door widened. The gypsum-toned stewardess with blue darted eyes shook as she stormed the Captain, Mr. Clinton.

"There is an Asian man I suspect to be sick!" Her quivering fingers intertwined.

"What? Where is he seated?" He hung up the radio call with pulled eyebrows.

"Seat CBE---Black-haired, medium-sized… and also Indian." She panicked.

"Communicate, it's mandatory to put on their masks, and also warn them about the disease again." His hands held hers tightly as she took a shallow breath to calm down. She then returned to the economy class, and her gloved palms held the mic for public announcements.

"Ladies and gentlemen, we advise and request that every passenger take precautions to wear their masks properly. Remember, good health is wealth." She spoke with a serious tone, awakening a lovely couple opposite me. Also, Jacqueline's hazel eyes watched me as I ran my dark-skinned fingers over my pale lips, yawning. It was such a long flight, but in my damn mind, I never planned to exclude anybody. I've always been excluded my entire life, and I knew how painful it felt. Maybe I should've been open to getting to know her.

I've been judged numerous times because of my flawless dark skin before I even opened my mouth. With these crazy labels of how I am supposed to behave or act, shoved down my dry throat. I wish they knew there was more to us than just made-up stereotypes.

Inside a low-slung building with this sealed wing labeled by a red warning light above the entrance, Dr. Sarah carried a portable PCR analyzer clipped on the Tvyek suit she wore while her gloved fingers manipulated sealed vials to check the formulas being formed to disinfect the disease. She seemed dissatisfied; the facts presented on the viral load graphs didn't make sense.

She walked out of the critical room for the observation chambers, sweat pooling down her angular face as Doctor Colton followed behind her. The atmosphere smelled faintly of ethanol, more like bleach fumes.

"What?" While she removed the white protective suit.

"We need to have the right formula."

He wrinkled the base of his nostrils.

"It's bullshit!" She clenched her not-sharp teeth, with cigarette fumes.

The man with salt and pepper hair pulled his rounded glasses off, short of words.

"You all haven't done enough." She blamed

him while these greenish muscles lay on her freckled forehead.

"Oh, come on. We should head back to Wuhan."

CHAPTER SEVEN

I badly wanted to fall in love with Chioma again. The long-distance aspect contributed to the walls we built between us. I missed our youthful secondary love and her sun-like smile that radiated warmth. But I wondered if I should be open to falling in love without judging by appearances, even though the main reason I wanted to reconnect with Chioma was for a cultural renewal.

I have changed as an African man who has lived half of my life in the States.

I hardly believed Chief Olubamise, her father, would like me since I had forgotten some of our key cultural norms. I mean, this Nigerian man rarely spoke proper Yoruba without adding two foreign words.

Also, I had reached the thirties, where I should've been open to whatever God has in store for me.

Ha-ha, I had gotten so old, but I believed if I had Chioma, I would totally be myself without over-explaining.

Anyway, the bruised skies with golden rays

hit Jasper in the tailored navy suit and earpieces, who monitored the façade entrance as Eleanor unlocked the frosted door, disabling alarms, and checking inventory while the crew in charge of cleaning came in, grabbing their yarned cloths and cinnamon-scented spray to polish the marble floors.

Also, she had morning paranoia and doubts about her sexual relationship with the security man who had beaten Jasper. Maybe she cared for him and never planned to cut him off as she swore to her little foster brother. Each step she took echoed like a respectful slow fat, not only that, but her rounded fingertips tingled with blue near her unkempt nails while her dry brown skin peeled off.

Her narrow chest grew heavy, causing her ribs to expand and contract in a frantic rhythm. She squinted her glassy eyes, coughing loudly as the two Dominican girls in charge of cleaning looked at each other with wide eyes, close to the private suits where pre-selected outfits awaited. Her quivering hand brushed her thin, smooth hair; unfortunately, she lost her balance and fell onto the marble floor.

In the cavernous terminal having an arched ceiling like careworn, ribbed with steel beams and dotted with skylights, this woman with slivery-white hair stood in a charcoal trench coat and button-down shirt. Beside her was Dr. Colton in a long-sleeved shirt tucked into the trousers to maybe cover the old tattoo on his wrist? While the floor was a polished stone and a waterproofed carpet, worn by millions of footsteps.

The air overlapped with sounds in the rhythmic clatter of rolling suitcases as they walked into a private jet. Her lean arm dropped the brown handbag on the floor. He stooped for her as she sat, buckling up. He took the firm seat facing her while he looked dead into her hazel eyes.

"I apologize; Okay?" He then avoided eye contact with her.

"You sure?" She had tensed jaws.

"I promise I'm going to be as professional as possible!" He reassured her.

"Apology accepted, now tighten your ass, I don't want us to be late."

He gasped in relief, lifting and relaxing his

not-young forehead.

Like I learned in today's America, I have to adapt and be tolerant of people's bad behavior without showing how it made me feel. Because my dark skin was the first reason strangers didn't trust me. My own survival was often at the expense of my master's well-being.

In the narrow hallway that contained cells with damp walls, peeling paint, and a foul smell, six demonstrators were dragged away and taken into custody. The two Jewish individuals and four people of color had been punched in their stomachs, and the youngest of them stumbled and begged for mercy on the dusty floor.

"I wish she would let me interrogate those niggas."

"Ha-ha, I know we would make them regret the day they were born."

These nonblack men in the navy blue police attire spoke their mind.

"Why would you say that?"

The three black women and one man had torn shirts, fresh bloody fibrous tissues on their full lips, and swollen brown eyes. One of the women with Afro hair had a twisted right foot, the mixed one with a gashed cheek, leaking with reddish residue, and the youngest, around sixteen years, trembled like an earthquake as her tiny hands were handcuffed too.

"Why are you being so aggressive?"

Of course, their subconscious hatred came to the forefront as they called the women any name, part of the son of God. These men, around forty-five years old, never cared to listen, as we've always been treated.

Very voiceless, and they made everything about themselves.

Like how dare you, black-y, to express your emotions! We minorities will never be given any grace to ever express the way we want to address our emotions. And that's a fact, yet *we love and care enough to listen to their concerns*. The moment we black people, especially dark-skinned women, speak, *we get shut down*.

We are *voiceless* every day.

We have to think of how to speak and act.

Because people like us are misunderstood, and we have to do a lot of explaining so they may care to pick up our concerns. And there are so many good white people in America and the world who have empathized with us for having to deal with that.

These men with pale skin barked like dogs as the poor Justin nodded his tiny head sideways. Their piercing hums worsened, and his laced boots walked like a thief, away from a crime scene. The shimmering lights flickered overhead, casting a pallor on the walls, slightly brownish from age, and stained past. He sat in the corner, cold and unforgiving, with his broad arms crisscrossed on his quivering chest.

Outside the window, the sky over Belgium was pale gray, struck with winter light, while an absolute absence of sound preoccupied every passenger; some of them held their arms close to their chests due to the fear of despair. And Le Floris and his other co-attendant moved with a quiet precision, checking latches and nodding to each other. Also, they gently woke the few passengers still leaning against the windows.

"Ladies and gentlemen, this is your captain speaking. We are now beginning our final descent into Zaventem airport. Local time is 1:22 pm, and the weather on the ground is partly cloudy with a temperature of 13 degrees Celsius. Please note that COVID-19 protocols are still in effect."

The air felt thinner, heavy with the scent of ethanol, and I adjusted my mask while my Indian neighbor squinted his glassy reddish eyes, but never dared to cough.

"We'd like to thank you for flying with us today. Please make sure your seatbelt is fastened, tray table is stowed, and all carry-on items are secure. Cabin crew, prepare for landing."

The engines shifted lower and more steadily, causing the plane to dip, and the industrial fields came into view—highways, the unmistakable layout of airport runways, and blinking lights. The enormous Airbus plane touched down on the ground while speeding forward.

CHAPTER EIGHT

The house of H & Z no longer whispered luxury, but smoked infectious pandemic. The ambulance blocked the flanked entrance, close to the sculptural planters where a well-styled doorman in a navy suit used to stand. The two medical men had Eleanor on the stretcher, fully dressed in PPE, as they administered oxygen through her nostrils.

"We'll swab before transport."

A not-young Middle Eastern lead doctor had them move with precision, and their exhales slightly fogged their clear plastic face shield in the process. Not only that, but they already had a bagged body in triple layers inside the ambulance. They placed her on the stretcher as they adjusted it; her reddish, grassy eyes became visible while they opened, alert and rimmed with tiredness.

In the far distance, she turned to see her little brother, Jasper, and her lips stretched into a smile. As it could be her last time, the boy stood still; his gaze was solemn, too still to understand his surroundings.

Perhaps he completely lost hope in life.

His silence cut deeper than a knife, no sign or reaction, absolutely nothing moved, and when the Ambulance set off, he came forth like a strike of thunder, running after her. These two detectives in button-down Charcoal shirts held him since they had to undergo the COVID-19 protocol.

"But I didn't tell anyone you were with him!"

His heart banged over one hundred thirty beats, with widened brows, and his eyes rolled out uncontrollable, colorless liquid.

He became petrified of losing her, and sudden paranoia built a home inside him. He bit his dark-skinned fingers as if he had lost trust in the system, and the haunting layer in the back of his tooth-shaped head worsened the entire situation.

"I know she will return…" His full-textured lips laughed like a madman. "She has to… She has always returned to me!"

This had awakened his senses that we were actually in the bad days, and he wished he could've done and learned more about her sister's relationship. Maybe confronting his workmate, Beom Seok, wasn't just good enough. It felt like when I realized I was a thirty-year-old Yoruba man without a wife, and I had these voices in my head that there must be something wrong with me.

Right? Because no one I loved showed romantic interest in me…

Even Chioma, I had to fulfill my promises first before she gave me a chance, and her love sometimes seemed so conditional to me. But I've been working and getting my life together. Oh, she would be my perfect match.

Inside the plane, we remained, where a six-foot-tall lady, dressed in a white Tyvek suit, approached us. She had on an N95 mask fogged with her breath as she walked row by row, scanning foreheads, collecting foams Le Floris had given, and asking questions in clipped English, Dutch, and French.

"You're welcome, our beautiful passengers. We would like to inform you that Belgium is under COVID-19 restrictions, as are the EU states at the moment. But since you're here, you will be quarantined for 7 days if we see your travel history in any high-risk territory as we wait for the way forward. Thank you!"

A quiet chatter and shuffling of our masks as we murmured around, regretting having taken the flight.

Also, a private jet's wheels met the Beijing tarmac with a muted thud through the haze of winter. No room for excitement as Doctor Sarah and Colton adjusted their masks speedily. She gazed at the sealed folder in her lap with a shallow breath. They walked out, and a pretty Chinese man with glassy skin in a suit approached them, his brown fingers pointed at a parked black van, since he seemed English illiterate.

She held the official clearance papers stamped by both the USA and China as they got in, and he drove off into an unspecified terminal. The air was dry, tingling with roasted chestnuts, the dense traffic, locals moved with purpose, masks on, but their gestures with warmth, and they passed through Shunyi District, with its gated parks and quiet suburbs to the north of the city, where a private facility far beyond the communities was built. Their staff dressed in PPE could be seen in the private quarters.

The two elderly men, dressed in Tyvek suits, approached the van while sanitizing to kill unnecessary viruses. The white doctors pulled out their personal sanitizers and rubbed them on their gloved fingers.

In a few minutes, the gate automatically opened as their Chinese driver continued into the facility. These heavily trained men monitored the fenced perimeters behind pine trees. It somehow looked like a simple University campus with white concrete walls, glass corridors, and a central courtyard with a koi pond.

Immediately, he parked, and a quick but composed brown nanoscopic lady dressed up in white PPE approached them as Doctor Sarah and Colton came out of the vehicle.

"Hello! I am Doctor Mel Ling. Welcome to Beijing!" She introduced herself with a bow and a clipboard.

"Nice to meet you as well." Doctor Sarah replied.

"It's my pleasure too." Colton joined with

his thicker voice.

"I'll escort you directly to the facility; we realized the disease late; it had already spread all over Wuhan." Mel Ling slumped her lean shoulders as these two elderly men came back while she moved them inside the gigantic laboratory with countless scientists having different samples and also made records of those unspecified body disorders.

"Well, how did it all start?" Doctor Sarah inquisitively asked.

The interior was partitioned into smaller rooms and sterilized from the quarantine wing to the BSL-3 certified labs, they equipped with virology, immunology, and genomic sequencing. While Doctor Mel Ling's dark brown eyes speedily blinked, as if she concealed or misrepresented the truth. I had seen those kinds of eyes on my traveling agent before.

"Our citizens just dropped dead in the hospitals. Coughing unnecessarily, so we aren't sure where it all began." She controlled her facial expression in such a deliberate intent, a little serious as she addressed the doctors.

Doctor Sarah gave her a shady eye of distrust, but she kept on smiling to keep it as professional as possible.

"All right then, guess I'm done here, let me check some samples down this side."

Mel Ling crossed her arms, avoiding eye contact, and walked, expelling air from her lungs heavily.

"I don't fucking believe her!" Doctor Sarah made her final remarks.

"Well---She's … I mean, she's a bit convincing." Colton stammered.

Dr. Sarah became quiet; perhaps she noticed his changed demeanor and how he may have looked at her.

The air was crisp outside, but thickened inside as my brain raced, not with panic, but with wonder if I would ever make it home to Chioma or even be able to see mama's grave. I had so many rituals to fulfill back home as my mind calculated, moreover, an hour since we had touched Dutch tilted soils.

My ears popped as the Congolese man gripped his scarf again, and the boy, around ten, kicked his short foot carelessly. Also, the white boy in a hoodie talked so loudly in Dutch on his earpieces that I looked back, even when we had maintained social distancing. I had already answered relevant questions as my broad, defined nostrils smelled her cinnamon and sage scent from behind before we even exchanged words.

"Oo chimoo, what?" I had a red-blue quickening breath as I adjusted my arms like I had massive wings.

She made me feel like a bird.

Maybe I had a thing for toxic women.

Or I was the problem.

"They're letting citizens go through."

Her lingering glances did some voodoo stuff to my inner human. I liked the way she smiled. Man, she had such a shimmering smile that melted inside, softening my soul. Maybe she could be open to learning my culture, but she was Dutch American, and I am African. I doubted she even cared since I never minded learning and having full-on conversations about the Dutch American culture existing in Pennsylvania.

"Why?" I inquisitively asked.

"They're citizens," Jacqueline etched close, into my 1.5 meters distance.

"All right then… good for them." I darted my sockets with an exhaustive tone.

She crisscrossed her pole-like arms, echoing my side eye, as she proceeded to walk away, but Jacqueline then returned even closer, holding my quivering, rugged arm.

"But you can come with me, okay?" She lowered her voice, becoming more intimate.

Maybe in love, differences in culture and appearance never mattered as long as whoever you love understands you. No matter what they look like or who they are or where they come from. As long as their presence feels like home. Or even culture.

"Okay!" She might've felt comfortable with me, and her tender touches were soft like cotton. I could see the corners of symmetrical lips as she smiled. We moved together through a widened door to another line heading to the immigration office.

CHAPTER NINE

A flickering bulb above the sinks outside buzzed as the two bodies inside the middle stall mingled in a hush, nose to nose, and lips to lips. They pounded, "Oh, yes!" The air was still reeking in ethanol and the scent of disinfectant as their gypsum blemish-free skins brushed each other.

Our gorgeous stewardess had sneaked in, with Captain Clinton, a much older man to her age, and he grasped her lean arms from the back, squeezing them cheeks, and her blue eyes shut in the process. The light spilled through the small gap beneath the door, staining his dry, full lips on her bigger ear. She turned her rounded face towards him while letting his cracked lips touch hers. His long, rough fingers pushed heavily inside her.

Her moisturized lips opened as she leaned in, and he widened her long, thick legs, letting the Captain ride her effortlessly.

Jacqueline and I had stepped out through the pale steel and breath-fogged glass. The skies were grey, and the air with a damp cold that clanged my eumelanin skin and rested into my narrow bones, but I still had visual flashes of Chioma, and I badly could not wait for the seven quarantine days to be done.

She was the girl I thought of before going to sleep and waking up. The only girl I craved for in my unattainable dreams, the lady of the second-largest continent, where my heart lay. I had zipped high my black jacket with a shabby quality, and my gloved fingers remained still since the temperatures were lower than we anticipated.

Jacqueline opted for a certified COVID-safe taxi where this masked man waved at us, and I rolled her purple suitcases with my black bag at once. I could see the city blurring my eyes as I dropped her stuff in the boot.

"You're stuck---with me here." Her deliberate pauses weaved these threads, no matter how hard I tried not to fall for her antics.

"*N'ezie!*"

"Of course!"

"Come on, let's go right now."

She held my hand. I would've bet a hundred dollars that no Abantu would believe me if I dared confess at home. We are so big on respect in Africa, so any lady who doesn't conform or fit in the category risks being cast out. The women who lead a man, at least, should lead with respect, especially around elders, not even love. Girls in Nigeria are a little shy and reserved; no way would they ever hold a man's hand.

Don't get me wrong, we Africans are very loving and friendly people, especially when you come into our culture. We love love, and loving on people, and we would show you everything about our mystical tribes.

But please, you have to lead with respect.

"I don't think it's a good idea." While I faced her banging chest, I heard these soft calls like transcendental music in my spine.

"I am not leaving without you," She crossed her arms with tensed jaws. "If you're staying, so am I."

I pulled my squared face away as she gave me a piercing eye, brief and playful.

She seemed so wild, and also a little intentional, mirroring her in my mind.

"I am coming with you, but please no

talking, at least this one journey."

She nodded without a word. Was she submissive? I couldn't tell as I pushed my handbag into the boot, also, I saw this not-young woman I suspected to be African in a bright wax-print dress who headed toward the escalator.

The virology wing on level two, behind biometric scanners and a double airlock system, was sterilized and cold, scrubbed by HEPA filters, and smelled faintly of latex while Dr. Sarah gave a side eye to Dr. Mel Ling, who lied to their faces and definitely broke their trust.

In the conference chamber, a long, centered table was set, with different Chinese doctors who discussed their research on the deadly disease. They all were in Tyvek suits, slightly fogged at the visor with black pens across their gloved hands.

"It causes a multi-organ involvement; I don't believe it came from the Wuhan market." Dr. Zhang, the chubbiest, stiffened his neck as he broke the ice of silence.

"I totally agree. It's too clean." May Ling

supported him? She seemed unsettled in the biometric chair while a translucent screen floated above the center, displaying their genomic sequences.

"That's a speculation. Do you have any sort of evidence to back it up?" Doctor Sarah asked eventually, as she leaned forward, narrowing her hazel eyes.

The silence fell into the dimly lit room, and everyone else fidgeted, including her travel partner, Dr. Colton.

"Or maybe there is no evidence because your government buried it." Her tone was satirical.

"I totally disagree with you, Doctor Sarah. But we all want the same thing. I think we should handle this pandemic 事情 like grown adults."

"Grown Adults? Many have lost their lives; it's a strong flu not to play with. It has demented our loved lives... broken our families apart." Dr. Sarah's eyes became reddish brown as she made her point to the entire Chinese board with a strained neck.

"What's your point?" Mel Ling swallowed a

gravel as she leaned back.

"I just lost my son…" She had droopy eyelids as Dr. Zhang tightened his jaw.

"A beautiful boy, he never hurt anybody in this lifetime. Yet he begged for more oxygen, and the hospital had none." The room seemed haunted with less warmth.

Her hands covered her rounded face with fixed muscles while this uncontrollable absence of sound preoccupied the board of twelve doctors.

"Now I'm on lithium as a broken mother thrown in such a treacherous transition, yet humanity needs me in this time. And I am so unhappy, but still here. Right?" She exhaled while her heavy voice cracked. Dr. Mel Ling gazed as her fixed finger was on the screen she held.

"I have not been sleeping, especially after his death, that's why I am on meds. And I refuse to be ashamed… just because I am on something doesn't mean I am not saving people's lives." She then stood walking around the center table in extreme despair.

CHAPTER TEN

Dr. Sarah had just been briefed by Dr. Zhang, one of the Chinese virologists, with slides displaying mutation clusters, vaccine drifts, and long COVID biomarkers inside a glass-walled room that overlooked the lab floor where they discussed different collaborations for their planned work. Not only that, she requested a bottle of water, and as he walked out, the skies were lit with faint neon lights and red lanterns, which she suspected came from the roadside eateries.

She waited until the last echoes of his footsteps faded and sipped in the viral sequencing room. The air reeked of ethanol and dust as she logged into the terminal using the identity card code he left on the rounded table and accessed data she shouldn't have. These restricted folders labeled CV-45 weren't on the official index she could access, and Dr. Sarah's fingers twitched on the keyboard. She opened them, tensing her chiseled jaw while her arm tucked her silky-white strand into the surgical cap she had on.

"WHAT?"

Inside, raw genomic sequences, timestamped July 23rd, 2019. She wiped her forehead with lines of confusion, as the strain was nearly identical to SAR-CoV-2 but named differently and less politicized. She cross-checked the sample ID and logged out immediately after hearing the old man's crunching footsteps.

On a top-floor labeled only for authorized personnel, there was a subterranean conference chamber. The white walls, equipped with monitors showing empty corridors, were soundproofed, and the atmosphere grew silent and tense.

Across Dr. Ling's biometric seat were three government officials: Vice Minister Chen Xiaohong, flanked by two not-young men in black suits with no name tags and their brown, rounded faces as hard as Mahogany wood carved from a stone. Her doggy face nodded her head sideways as he addressed her.

"You were supposed to convince them--- very simple!" The chief military officer raised his hoarse voice. In his combat-laced boots, he stood forward, walking step by step, and circling her like a predator. From nowhere, his rugged hand grasped a fistful of her black hair, twisting it cruelly.

"Ouch!" She made loud wails as he jerked her head back until her rounded neck arched.

"You think you're better than us?" He sizzled. "Okay, do you really think you matter than your own country's survival?"

She tightened her textured lips without a word, and he blew an open palm, sharp and loud, exploding heat on her reddish cheekbone. Her scalp burned, but she refused to open her mouth.

"Make it right... There shall not be a next time."

Inside a COVID-19 treatment ward, the once-bustling general hospital wing had turned into a high-risk isolation zone where temperatures hovered just below comfort, cool enough to slow microbial spread, however, too cold to rest. Eleanor sobbed for a minute as her reddish eyes landed on numerous deathbeds all over the place. These hums of oxygen-concentrators, infusion pumps, and portable ventilators filled the space. Even her heartbeats were monitored, and she became hopeless.

The fluorescent lights buzzed overhead as she forcefully pulled her tiny arm with too much strength to cover a body that was no longer alive, but in the process. She barely recognized her pale, cracked hands stained with shades of blue. Her heart pounded in her chest as she gradually pulled the neighbor's sheet away from his face.

His monitor displayed his zero percent oxygen saturation like a haunting sight, and she kept her mouth shut while crying out at the same time. Phillip's corpse was right in front of her. He had died, and she was drowning in misery. The nurse nearby approached her while inserting a benzodiazepine into her IV, causing her to lose consciousness.

During a peaceful demonstration along a tree-lined street in the Mission District, Americans wearing masks walked with discontent toward the police, holding signs expressing their dissatisfaction with the rapid deaths caused by this unknown pandemic. Suddenly, the air turned contaminated with teargas that stung their skin and blurred their vision. An elderly African American man, around sixty-two years old, stumbled while clutching his handmade sign saying, 'Black Lives Matter,' as sweat and smoke enveloped them.

The police struck their tightly laced boots in the same pitch, percussively warning the protesters. Their shields glinted under the harsh floodlights, forming an impenetrable wall, pushing them away mercilessly with their emotionless faces behind the visors.

Justin had remained in the car, the police lady noticed, and she quickly approached him.

"What are you doing?" She pulled her well-knitted brows with a red-blue temper.

And poor Justin got onto his black shiny boots, looking away from her distressed face.

"I'm not participating!" His raspy voice came in a low tone as one of the officers raised his baton, swinging it towards a brown woman in a Hijab who was retreating already.

"What have you just said?" She couldn't believe her ears at the time.

"I am not well." He assured her.

"What? Are you sure?" The Sheriff seemed unsettled, as if she wanted him not to accept her persuasion.

His chocolate eyes gazed, seeing what had become of the police, the illicit treatment, and unfairness done since this woman pleaded for mercy as a blow landed with a thud onto her chubby cheeks.

"Yes---I am sure... I can't do it." His voice cracked as he noticed the whites of her eyes, but she quickly blushed it away.

"All right then, you're free to go home."

"For real?"

"Yes, and please don't come even tomorrow. I will cover for you." She assured him.

A white mother shielded her mixed-race son, who looked about sixteen, as she crouched beside a toppled barricade, trembling like an earthquake. His eyes were wide open, especially regarding what was happening; he wondered how ironic the police had become. Instead of listening and understanding the civilians' concerns, they crushed them.

These people had lost their uncles, sisters,

brothers, mothers, grandparents, friends, and many loved ones; they needed comfort, reassurance, and to hear that everything would be okay. That's all — the disgust on Justin's face said it all.

CHAPTER ELEVEN

The circular striking structure with wooden seats in the rows was packed with people I had never known. And the atmosphere was brittle like weak, shattered glass since the rain had fallen an hour before, leaving the long pavement from the church slick, and the skies bruised gray. Mourners in masks filed in slowly, the two married women held their umbrellas in a loose semicircle, and the crowd was mixed with two lawyers in suits from the Belgian immigration office.

A brunette lady in a tailored black suit and a crimson head wrap stood still. Her soaking wet eyes had turned reddish. Her black heels were too low, perhaps distressed for knowing so much about me. Her shaking fingers intertwined as a man in a black liturgical vestment honored the funeral ceremony in the backyard.

'She could've met someone else. Like a banker or diplomat, someone part of us.'

'Her mother never liked the boy; this is going to be interesting.' She could listen to

what these married women said, as her chest grew heavier than usual. She had trouble breathing as her arm ran through her swollen, reddish eyes.

"May his soul rest in Peace---our departed Ahmed Olaoluwatomijogun?"

The redhead religious leader struggled to read my name in front of his audience.

Ahmed adored his culture, believed in Nigerian traditions, and always dreamt of resting beside his mother.

"Oh, stupid girl." This six-foot woman with glassy skin, who had stood several feet away, dressed in a cream trench coat and leather gloves, approached her daughter in despair.

"No, mama, no! You didn't even like him."

"Ha-ha." She made spontaneous sounds out, trying to kill this inorganic energy as every eye was on them, "She's just emotional, everyone, never mind her."

"Don't act as you did, all of you didn't even know him!" Her voice rose, making a massive mess.

We had just gotten a car that smoothly carried us through Brussels. The city welcomed me with gentle drizzles, not quite rain or mist. The cobblestones sparkled like diamonds on the wide boulevard roads near the station. The Dutch people wore woolen coats with masks on as the car parked near a tall hotel, where bicycles zipped past puddles.

My arm reached into my pockets for some of my savings I had to pay, and she insisted, but I refused. The way we African men are raised, especially in Nigeria, is that a woman does not have to pay for anything in front of a man.

In fact, there's a level of respect and honor that comes with a supportive man. We're there for protection, emotional support, and financial stability. So, I couldn't let it happen on my watch. It wasn't morally right in my Yoruba culture, and I moved out of the car with dreamy eyes, carrying our luggage from the trunk.

We stepped inside, and the frosted door closed with a thud as we moved toward a small lobby where two men in suits quickly took our luggage. The middle-aged lady slouched in her seat, and her rounded arms typed on the keyboard.

"You're welcome, please." The five-feet-three-inch tall lady ignored me. At home, we're strong on being a man's world, and this would've never happened. Differences in our cultures, I guess—in Nigeria, she would never have even looked at the bill in public.

"Yes, thanks." She replied.

"You have reservations?"

"But I think we may need another room?"

Jacqueline's hazel eyes avoided mine, and I grew restless as she leaned in, accidentally brushing my gloved hand, with her lean arms crisscrossed.

"Or we could share mine, I don't mind." She refused to give me polite grins, but these full smiles exposed her sharp, pearly teeth, and I became petrified; she would make a man do crazy things to her.

"I mind." I clenched my jaw as I pulled my squared face away.

"Pride and victimization have always been their go-to whenever we try to help".

I never understood what the receptionist meant. But since I lived in the Western world, I realized that women here, especially African

Americans, never submit or are allowed to be silenced, which I respected.

Because they were raised to be independent, and in case my brothers aren't acting right, they would give them some 'BLACK ATTITUDE.'

Which is also a terrible stereotype

Was her statement either gender or race-focused? I wondered as the chubby lady made low comments.

"What did you just say?" Jacqueline had droopy eyelids, down-turning the corners of her moisturized, bowlike lips. She parched her forehead, and this woman slouched her plumpy shoulders again, brushing them off like a silly joke.

"Please, just stop." I interrupted.

"We shall share the room!" I had never been respected by an owl anyway.

Jacqueline's furrowed face stared in front with these colorless liquids in her eyes. She pursed her lips again when she looked at her, nodding her head with distaste. We walked to the hallway as the light faded, and when she opened the room, the amber glow embraced us like candlelight.

Inside the joint research facility located in Changping District, north of the city, this man with salt and pepper hair examined tissue samples from the recovered patients with his gloved hands, and the data flowed. Also, the city pulsed outside with a young night; however, within the concrete walls, time was measured in viral load sequences.

In silence, he then heard the hums of footsteps filtered in the air, and distant clicking from Dr. Zhang in the other wing. He remained still, pursing his small, dry lips and looking back from time to time.

"Hey!" She raised his heartbeats, and he hunched his flat back, walking out of the glass walls of the center technical lab and removing the Tyvek suit.

"What?" He ground his teeth.

"She lied to us all!" Her fistful arms leaned forward aggressively in the air.

"Really?"

He looked away with minimal movements.

"For REAL?" Dr. Sarah's balanced nose flared in the process. "You don't believe me. Do you?"

"No, I am LISTENING so I may give my opinion for once."

He invaded her space, and his shallow breath hit her freckled forehead with jerky motions like a madman in love.

"Totally---she lied to our faces." He tensed his sharp jaw, and she swallowed her relief.

Outside the cobbled street in a suburban neighborhood, stood a house with a wrought-iron balcony among many others, tall windows draped in linen, and a tiled foyer in patterned stone where our Captain entered past 4 pm. The heavy door clicked shut behind him as a redheaded woman quickly approached him. The walls had portraits of their lovely son for around six years.

She removed his tailored navy wool trench, which hung on his broad shoulders; he had worn a cashmere turtleneck, slim-cut trousers in slate gray, and overly polished leather shoes. He looked too deliberate---the kind that whispered influence without a word.

"I can smell her on you." She furrowed her forehead in disbelief while her arm struck his pectorals. He held her tightly while she made wails of pain, "That perfume. Not mine or yours."

"I can explain." Clinton paused, unbuttoning his coat slowly, as if he bought time.

"Well, don't." She scoffed. "It's okay?"

"We only had a drink… that's all."

"Oh, there we go again, see Clinton … I am very exhausted. May I go to sleep?"

The whites in her eyes said it all as the tension crackled; she didn't want to be part of the entanglement with his other woman. While her feet tried to walk away, this man went on his knees.

"I want you so much."

"No, you don't!"

"Think about our son before you make any decision."

His jaw clenched.

"Like the way you thought about him when you screwed your stewardess."

"It was only a drink."

"Yeah, for sure." The room with its velvet curtains and modern, structured antique seemed to shrink around them, as she quickly walked away into their bedroom, and shut the wooden door on his ghostly face. Her flared nose expelled air as teardrops rolled out of her brownish eyes.

"Shit!" Clinton's well-built arms struck the door, and he began throwing the family's framed portraits off the corridor of the white wall. She held onto her textured lips as if she fought for her life. The hallway became a disarray while he paced around like an immature man.

CHAPTER TWELVE

February 3rd, 2020

In a narrow corridor, with low throbs of refrigeration units embedded in the walls, and the ethanol air smelled like a bloody birth on steel. Gleaming lights cast a pallid sheen on the polished floor while Dr. Zhang suddenly stood from his seat, wiry and stepped into the hallway with precision, his brownish eyes keeping a steady gaze on Dr. Sarah, who was concentrating on the last lab graph sequence.

His lab coat was crisp as he scrubbed; his eyes, behind the rectangular glasses, darted left and right as he settled in the camera with a nod. Not only that, Dr. Mei Xiu, a much younger doctor, followed behind him. And her small hands clutched on a tablet, and the screen dimmed, but the glow remained beneath her thumb. Also, Dr. Chen, the still grieving doctor, noticed certain virologists leaving the laboratories in a worrying way. She breathed out heavily from her lungs as she followed Doctor Xian.

Inside a sealed isolation ward, 6:43 AM, the

walls were pale green, scrubbed clean. However, stained with hopelessness and red-blue suffering scuff marks from gurneys. The still Persian nurse in the N95 mask had leaned Eleanor's forehead in exhaustion.

She lay in the middle of the room, barely present beneath the tangle of tubing and wires. Her frowning face had cracked lips, and her entire body had shrunk in the past day, muscles gone, and skin sagging against her bones. The ventilator loomed beside her, and pulsing with numbers of respiratory rate below the average.

This reminded me of my mama's situation.

I was going to work when Dr. Chukwuemeka called to inform me about Mama's death. It was heart-wrenching since I did not get a chance to say goodbye to her. And I asked myself how long life shall last for me to see her… I missed her so much, and I still do. However, the only thing that flamed courage back to my soul was the promises I made of marrying and starting up a happy family she never had a chance to ever experience.

The nurse set the tablet on the stand, angled

toward her pale face, and the screen showed the man of God, Father Curry, seated in a quiet chapel, lit by candlelight. He also wore a white stole, and his clean-shaven face was lined with empathy and age.

"What's your name, child?" He brought a sudden warmth into the dim room.

"El…e…nor!" She tried to open her ghostly lips.

"Child! God will bless you---with HIS gracious blessings."

"I'm… scared."

Truly, grief doesn't wait for anyone. However, there's always growth and strength in being able to accept the unacceptable, especially for the things we have no control over.

Like life or death.

"No matter what happens… I am here with you!" Her reddish eyes fluttered open, even though she couldn't say a word. Her narrow, bony cheeks placed a simple smile on her face as she made longer, sharper coughs thoroughly.

Sometimes sad tears are happiness;

however, we need to show up for our workmates, families, friends, or even our neighbors. We've no idea what they're going through.

The chandelier on the ceiling glittered coldly, casting fractured light across the marble. The Captain's house with velvet drapes and framed family art, some still on the floor, and bottles of beer lying beneath his feet. He received a call that awakened him on the black sofas. His big arms stretched while he yawned and then checked the phone.

He tensed his chiseled jaw, darting his eyes on the foyer while he sat hunched on the edge of the couch.

"I miss you." This soft, intimate sound, almost rehearsed, came out of the call.

"You don't call when I'm with my family." His widened eyes looked everywhere as the colorless liquid pooled out of his skull.

"What? I am your family too---I guess I should remind you I am with child."

His left leg bounced nervously, tapping against the floor in a staccato rhythm.

"I am going to be the mother of your child. I

deserve to be respected as well."

She demanded careful consideration while his free hand gripped the armrest, and his knuckles paled. He swallowed up his thick saliva while breathing out.

"I am sorry." The corners of his lips softened with lines of amusement. "You're my family too."

"Really?"

"Yeah." But the smile did not reach the eyes.

"Okay, the apology is accepted." Her voice became higher as she spoke.

"So when are you coming back here? We miss you." She asked eventually.

His white fingers touched the back of his head, distressed while looking at the closed door. Maybe the guilt hit him terribly, the humiliation he had caused his wife. And his gaze flickered toward the hallway every now and then.

"What do you mean? I am supposed to self-quarantine."

His broad shoulders tensed, rising with each breath, and then dropping.

"You find any excuse not to see the mother

of your future daughter!"

He leaned forward, his narrow elbows on the quivering knees, trying to fold himself away. Maybe to hide away from the yielded fruits of infidelity.

"Of course not, I'll see you."

His left arm traced the rim of the halfway bottle of beer.

"If you don't make it here, I am coming there for you." She threatened, "So you either choose your future baby mother or your crazy wife." She hung up on him.

The walls had been painted with a soft dusty cream, almost like parchment, in the room I shared with a pretty lady, whose eyes searched my square face with hunger. Around the wooden four-sided couch we shared, tinged with hibiscus scent, and my arms held a DualShock controller, playing video games on the screen, totally ignoring her. However, she leaned forward slightly, her elbows resting on the table, not only that, but her chin tilted, drawing my eye.

"What scares you?" Her fingers traced the rim of the teacup absently on the table, and her brunette hair was loosely pulled into a bun, with strands falling around her temples.

"What?" I retreated, and my pole-like legs crossed beneath the table.

"Life scares me. How about you?"

"Being misunderstood."

She reached across my left leg, and her soft fingers brushed me.

"I cannot afford to be misunderstood, especially in America."

I was not cognizant of race before I left Africa. It wasn't a relevant problem we faced. Until I realized even when I am Nigerian, I'm black in America. Because race is such a social construct. And in American society, everything we do or may not have access to is based upon our race.

And they do have owls, or I should call them gatekeepers, who carry on the legacy of racism and actively benefit from the most egregious parts of white supremacy, from the most vivid displays of violence against black people and the normality of it in these days and ages.

CHAPTER THIRTEEN

In the center of a dimly lit operations room, the air had become so cold, and the walls shook due to the ongoing tension around the circular table where ten Chinese doctors met. The screen was stained with raw genomic sequences, July 23rd, 2019. Also, Dr. Sarah minimized the window to have a clear view without being seen.

Dr. Zhang leaned forward, his voice low and sharp.

"But we've reviewed your internal logs." Dr. Mel Ling slant tablet toward him.

"Your team sequenced a strain labelled CV-45."

His shoulders slumped and eyes hollowed immediately he checked.

"This can't come out in the press!"

Dr. Chen's eyes flicked while his shoulders rose slightly, alert.

"It was an anomaly. We flagged it for further analysis. The sample was destroyed per protocol."

"No. Dr. Zhang." Dr. Mei Xiu, with a

mutton-chopped beard, opened his textured lips for the first time. "This is beyond scientific comparison. It's not the same."

"Do you know what's at stake?" Dr. Mel tightened her jaw, "If this data leaks, it will be taken as evidence of concealment. Or worse."

He remained still, and a complete absence of sound occupied them; also, his eyes were on Mel, very unmoved on the matter. Perhaps thinking about the consequences of their actions.

"Your notes suggested that it was viable. Transmissible, comparing it to SAR-CoV-2."

"But you sent me here to find answers, not bury them."

"It isn't about deletion but discretion." She swallowed a lump in her throat.

"And also revise the narrative. Say the sample was contaminated or misclassified. You understand, say anything else other than the truth."

Dr. Mei stood up suddenly while clearing her throat to be audible.

"We need to cover our country."

"I don't know." His rounded fingers

intertwined on the table while the room even became quieter than usual.

"We're not asking, but informing you."

"YOU'RE THREATENING ME?"

"No, Uncle… Just do it." She held onto his quivering hands on the table.

"I… I can't."

He rose while everyone else remained still on the biometric seats.

"You don't want to leave."

"Oh, what?" He slouched his shoulders while walking toward the door.

Dr. Mel Ling faced the blank wall, maybe calculating her next move.

These two men in suits grasped the chubby doctor by the collars of his lab coat, shoving him against the wall, and his rounded face hit the concrete with a dull thud.

"Do you really think you're untouchable?" Dr. Mel Ling never turned.

He clenched his brown teeth, pulling his eyebrows together, and reddish residue leaked from his temple. Dr. Sarah shook behind the glass window as she listened also their cold voices also became lower. She took a shallow breath, made up her mind, and walked away.

The ceiling was low, and intimate with exposed wooden beams, and a faint hum of air conditioner blended with the muffled sounds from the traffic outside, barely audible through the double-glazed window of the hotel. The queen-sized bed was dressed in white cotton sheets and two pillows stained with our strands. Jacqueline hunched onto the edge where I lay, right to a narrow wardrobe with mirrored doors, and I had a massive heartache.

Not only that, her curved back straightened, but rigid, opening up her body for me. Her knees uncrossed, and one of her pretty toes brushed my side as I bit the sides of full, textured lips. Her blouse was linen, pale white, and with several folds from the day; my goodness, she was such a candlelight in our dim room. I rose, sitting across her, and my hairy pole-like legs apart. She rested her tender elbows on mine, and her hands loosely clasped my extended goatee beard.

My upper chest rose and fell in a subtle tension, and I had this quiet intensity with her. She ate my symmetrical lips with passion, thundering me down, and I widened my brownish eyes. She was three thousand two hundred and fifty times sweeter than katemfe.

She held my rugged fingers on her thick thigh, and my thumb rubbed against her, her hazel eyes half-closed while I bit her rounded neck, all the way over her lean chest, she exhaled, and rolled her sockets.

"Please."

Jacqueline begged me.

The cell doors creaked open, metal on metal cold across the damp hallway where the concrete boxes had rusted bars and stained floors that stripped the dignity of the four African American men they dragged inside. Their clothes hang loose, torn from the scuffle. The one with braids limped, missing one of his sneakers, and his socks used to be white socks soaked in blood.

"LET US BE BLACK IN PEACE!"

His raspy voice cracked, as the other three joined him, these nonblack police men had used their 'practiced aggression', pushing their elbows and knees onto their backs. And for me, this was the reason why I only identified being black in America, because using 'Nigerian', which is my nationality, structured the system where owls benefited. And I would've actively kept up their structures that enabled them to get away with such acts.

The not-young officer had even shoved the teenage boy against the table as they dragged them from the Mission District. And his forehead hit the metal with a dull thud. The boy kept on shouting, 'I didn't do anything,' but his words vanished into his ears.

Because, truly, if 'racism was so bad' as they claimed, we wouldn't have such a climate in America today.

If racism were so egregious as they said, we would've packed this up a long time ago. PERIOD! If you truly think it's not a problem in America, it doesn't affect you. So, as a Nigerian who used to have a few understanding of racism within the context of American society, I wouldn't minimize the degree, severity, and depth of black Americans' history in conjunction with what the owls have intentionally orchestrated against them.

SORRY, BUT … I'M DIFFERENT

CHAPTER FOURTEEN

February 4th, 2020

The light filtered through gauzy curtains, casting pale gold across the bedspread. A landscape of our skin tangled in sheets, half on the floor, and the other across her hip and my sculpted shoulder, while we lay naked and still warm. We had sexually soul tied, and her blemish-free back was on me; I could feel more than her curved spine gleaming with light shades like a sculpture.

And my rugged hand rested on the dip between her smooth shoulder blades, a little possessive though. I had never experienced being made love to, the rightest way, like I did that night, not tentative but certain and intentional. Every touch from her was a million times meaningful and logical. Maybe because she knew where to move me, and the air became so thick. I had to show her some of my God given and hidden talents.

God! I was such a bad boy…

The things I may have done to her. I had no idea where I got the balls to even look into her hazel eyes. To have her see me in ways I never knew were possible without armor scared me. Like I was running for my life. Her brunette hair smelled of lavender and was still with colorless liquid. Also, we could hear the city moving in slow motion, but we did not want to leave each other for even a second. She felt like a divine gift I had always yearned for.

Maybe she was a sign or not.

Maybe love came in forms we never knew.

From the unexpected.

Maybe not…

In the white concrete building, her balanced nostrils kept catching ethanol air while she walked into the BSL-3 lab, full of silence, apart from the hums from her distant footsteps. Her workmate examined new tissue samples from two recovered patients in his gloved hands, and he recorded data. Dr. Lin, who was seated behind Dr. Colton, was immersed in the picture of her lovely daughter on her laptop. Dr. Wei, a much older man, noted his findings, close to her, but with quiet diplomacy, and sometimes they only nodded to one another.

The rain had begun to fall, soft and

persistent like a whisper on the roof. The wind carried the scent of distant smoke as Dr. Sarah reached him, sitting on the biometric seat, but dressed in an N95 mask, and also black, shabby trousers.

"They know." She made low sounds that he barely could hear, and her hazel eyes scanned their backs immediately after a soft chime sounded from a biometric reaction from Dr. Wei's samples.

"What?" He widened his eyes while hunching on the seat.

"Yes." Sarah gave him a serious tone that assured him.

"You guys are working too early." Dr. Lin interrupted them from nowhere.

"We are trying to… to model zoonotic spillover." Whatever creativity universe she got the response from, it actually worked since Dr. Lin seemed confident in her words.

"All right. There you go."

She retreated with a massive smile while Dr. Sarah moved Dr. Colton toward the hallway. Her wiggling arms still leaked with the colorless sweat of what she may have watched going down.

"I found folders in the archive – 2019 on Dr. Zhang's laptop." She took a deep breath as her eyes looked left and right in the corridor. "A few entries were timesstamped as far as July 23rd, but their metadata shows they were created in March 2020."

"What?" He pulled away his face with lines of age and wonder.

"Yes, they're backdated samples." She crisscrossed her arms as Dr. Colton began fidgeting, and his gloved hand touched his slightly wet neck.

"They're having a special meeting excluding us. Doesn't that ring a bell in your head?"

To the right, a man in his sixties lay prone, his body turned face down for the expansion of his lungs, while to his right was a much younger woman in her thirties. Her reddish brown eyes shut, lashes damp, and her lean chest rose and fell with the rhythm of the ventilator. Between them, a third patient stirred, coughing into the mask, and his eyes darted toward the weak Eleanor. In the corner, the Persian nurse received the doctor's reviews, her rounded face lined, and her eyes had rimmed in red.

She gave her the vial of Remdesivir to stabilize her; each breath she took came with a soft mechanical sigh, followed by a pause, then another sigh. It sounded almost maternal, except for the alarm that chirped every few minutes.

The nurse propped the tablet on the stand beside her bed, angled toward her pale face. The screen showed a young African American man in his early twenties, Jasper, who ran his hands to his soaking wet eyes from time to time, drowning in misery.

She had lain slightly on one side, though the position was dictated not by comfort, but by the tubes that threaded in and out of her body.

When her eyes fell on her little foster brother, he broke, piece by piece. God, we all hated these times, and his widened eyes glanced at her bony face. Her bones were visible. As her apart, dry and cracked lips slightly stretched the corners.

"Jasper… my little star…"

"I've been missing you every day." He cried while biting his lip, trying not to sob in front of her. Eleanor's dry fingers twitched against the blanket, and her voice was barely audible.

"I am so sorry, sister." He blew his broad nostrils in the process, while these green muscles were displayed on his forehead. "I'm sorry."

"I see us… when we were young." A long pause occurred, and the monitor began beeping steadily. Eleanor's eyes drifted closed, then opened again, but slower this time.

"SISTER STAY WITH ME!" His raspy voice hit sharp as the nurse asked him to tone it down. The oxygen mask fogged her face, and he could barely see her now, but Eleanor's lips moved silently, echoing words he could not hear like talking to a brick wall.

"Eleanor? Eleanor? Please stay, I love you. I love you so much." His hands were all over his full, textured lips, and he stepped back from his phone in extreme fear of losing her. Eleanor's eyes fixed on the screen one last time, and her mouth pulled so much echo, 'Love you.'

The monitor flatlined, as Jasper stared so cold, and his quivering hands reached toward the screen, as if he could even touch her face through the glass. Sometimes we become stronger in the worst times, when we are not in control of the unexpected. His big lips pressed together, then parted in a silent cry, the one with haunting despair, and also the lamp next to him, flickered like they could feel his excruciating pain. The siren walls in his background shook with the swaying winds. "You're my everything, Eleanor… All I have it's you."

CHAPTER FIFTEEN

The time I lived in the States, I heard different conspiracies from American women on how their families would feel when they dated us, Africans. I cared to know, not that I planned to date them, anyway, but because mama and I were so big on family since we yearned to build a massive bloodline she never got a chance to have. She always lawyered for me for her grandchildren, but of course, after marriage in the States.

I remember one time, this beautiful Afro woman said in the church that her family likes to tease, and they may make fun of our accents, which was funny and insightful.

The other not-so-young lady with a massive hat said they would only tell her to make sure she knows how many wives we may have, which I couldn't defend. I mean, our culture is so diverse, but if a man can provide for four wives, why can't he keep them all?

Pretty Jacqueline lay beside me, and her smooth arm loosely across my waist as I felt her breath, steady and warm against my sculpted shoulder. This severe silence of intimacy between us elapsed, and her thick thighs tangled on mine. We faced each other as we turned; she was such a beautiful woman.

She still is…

Such a tasteful woman.

And when she smiled, her pearly teeth blurred my sight, like a new man in love. No words would ever justify how she made me feel. Like a man, I had not felt like one for quite some time, especially the years I spent in the States. Also, the Dutch in her physical touches needed to be investigated. Her fingertips held so much power to inflict influence over me. I never used to be soft or settled the way I was with her.

And I had these unattainable dreams in my mind while her snowy hand brushed my sheepish hair from my squared forehead. A long peck pressed to the curve of my shoulder defrosted my soul, and I craved for more. This invisible bubble between us shrank, and I had a feeling she wanted to eat me alive.

But I never once fidgeted or glanced away at what may have come from a grim presence. We shared a breath, nose to nose, held a gaze while she ate my full, textured lips as if she licked strawberry ice cream. Super smooth, we moisturized our mouths with both vanilla and chocolate flavors. I would never forget how she tasted, so full of bergamot orange juices, peeled and blended in a sugar syrup.

She was such a citron tree. Her hand on my bulky back as she navigated a crowd of my inner self.

"Who are you when no one's watching?"

She brightened her face, but not to deflect, "I'm someone who calls her mother every weekend. That leaves parties early to control my drinking issues, and also afraid of being too much or not enough, like in my previous relationship."

Her eyes became slightly wet as my hand ran to dry off the leaking sides.

"You're more than enough---not for me or anyone but yourself."

She placed her hand in mine, and her fingers were cool, and I warmed them up.

"I'm someone who still dreams in Yoruba."

I said, and I watched her laugh so loud.

Mission accomplished.

Her smiles were genuine, like a pen on paper, and anyone could read each word in her sunning face.

"I'm a man who still writes letters to my secondary girlfriend who never responds." My raspy voice came in the low growing of this tension between us. "That has so much love but is afraid of being loved for the wrong reasons." My jaw softened as she looked at me, not for flaws but for my history.

The subterranean secret meeting chamber had dimmed, with humming tension among the ten Chinese Doctors. She stood alone amidst chaos inside, her lab coat buttoned to the throat, and rigid with defiance. Across her was Dr. Zhang, who spat reddish residue to the floor as this thick air recycled his silence.

"You're making this worse for yourself." Dr. Mel Ling scraped her seat against the floor with rage.

"You challenged my human values and things I believe in with my cowardice."

The room became quieter than usual as Dr. Chen folded his hands again for a third time in a row.

"And for the first time, I choose."

"ENOUGH! He is not the only one who knows."

"What!" The hum of noises from the doctors rang like bees with intense hand movements, and some hunched on their biometric seats.

"Can you shut up?" Her hand thundered the rounded table for everyone's eye.

"I'll find them." She clenched her jaws while Dr. Sarah shook like an earthquake, and as she speedily walked, with a red-blue temperature, the double wooden door opened. She trembled but was not broken, and her warm breath came in a shallow.

Not only that, but Dr. Mel walked toward her while she stood across the door, and she shimmered her sharp, honey-like skin as she approached the white corridor, close to the labs.

"How would you feel?"

She narrowed her hazel eyes while tapping her foot.

"Delightful, I suppose."

Dr. Mel's voice was heavier than usual, and

her brownish eyes lacked soul, which stiffened Dr. Sarah. She crossed her arms, and Mel turned away from her, but before she left, Sarah stopped her. She almost pulled away, without any suspicions until then.

"I looked into some reviewed sequence." Mel tightened her jaws. "Labelled BA-42 on December 25th, 2020." She then took a breath of relief, with a sudden surprise.

"I couldn't find the strain in the public records before. Do you mind explaining?"

"I don't understand how that happened."

"Really? Now you're playing games--- Look, people are out there dying, but you have the nerves to lie in our faces." She rolled her narrowed sockets while Dr. Mel ran her brown arm, tucking hair behind her ear.

"No, I didn't. Maybe they flagged it for further analysis. I have no idea, man."

The nine doctors began coming out of the chamber, turning their attention towards them. And she remained still, calculating her next move. Dr. Sarah realized she was alone, and her silence was the only option since Dr. Zhang never came out of that room.

"Hey!" She snapped out of her haunting thoughts. "You need to get back to work."

Mel Ling raised her voice at her Chinese colleagues as well, who stared at them.

"I don't know where you're coming from with this wrong information. Perhaps from the lithium or grief." Her whispers sliced like a knife, and she wondered how people could go so low.

The air thickened, and tear gas hissed amidst a screaming man, Beom Seok, curling into his reddish brown eyes, and dry, parted lips. He and the other protestors coughed inside their masks, retched, and stumbled. A young lady around fifteen with braids ran blindly with her chocolate arm, holding a sigh, 'Is my brother next?' Their arms outstretched, as she called for her elder brother with a circle beard. The existence of racism depended upon how we, black people, no matter where we come from, speak up for ourselves. In this event, speaking alone could have eradicated racism, and her voice became shallow due to the chaos.

Not made by the crowd, no, but the police. A ripple motion, so fast and rehearsed, emerged. And their shields lifted, and batons angled. The front row of officers surged forward on a tree-lined road in the Mission District, lanced boots pounding like drums.

Beom Seok, in a navy blazer, never flinched, raising his brown arms in search of oxygen, but the blow came sideways, catching his ribs. He folded with narrowed eyes like a tree stuck at the base while these reddish residues puddled. He fluttered down, landing in a bloody path of this fifteen-year-old girl that hadn't yet dried out.

Justin drove the police car, checking around the neighborhood. His visual series deeply carried away, when he turned ten years old. In the disarray condominium, in Castleberry Hill, Atlanta. His little self, with massive sheepish hair, walked into the bloody bathtub, a small glass container with white powdered crack spread around. The raining showers became louder, flowing lots of water, inside a Jacuzzi, his eyes became reddish brown, and he ran his quivering fingers onto his open mouth. His heart pounded over a hundred beats while he pulled her bloody hand, trying to awaken her.

"Mommy? Mommy? Please wake up, mommy! Mommy!" He cried.

His mind came forth from horrifying memories while he met a medium-sized man, dressed in police attire, striking forcibly his foot onto the young lady with skin like coffee, on a small dark pavement between two households. He pulled his brows in despair while hunching inside his seat. He parked the car across the shallow road and quickly opened up his benzodiazepine meds. He took two pills with shades of blue, trying to escape his present and past.

I used to believe things would change if we had Black representations in major offices, but oh well, nothing really changes in this country. Still, having Black Americans represented is always a good thing, but not a revolutionary act, especially if that representation only happens strategically or only occasionally. It wasn't progress for him to cry in the car, fight, and struggle for a crumb in these past eleven months since he officially joined the police department.

But a cycle of pacifying and attempting to

indirectly further the closeness to the root of the matter. Right?

CHAPTER SIXTEEN

Within our community, there are black people, especially fellow Africans, when they speak of racism, it's like an entire part of the story and idea. Maybe that's why we're still here today—bruised and broken. Why is there no side of the story where we see them for who they are and how diabolical they've been?

I am talking about people who have drowned and set towns on fire, dragging black people outside of their houses two and three in the morning. Not only that, but they were tied to crosses and burned alive. Tying them to railroad tracks and leaving them to be...

They say a Yoruba man can't cry, but I become teary whenever I remember what they did. And when I hear some of our flocks minimizing racism, it's like negating our obstacles completely. More of an attempt to turn a blind eye to the fact is due in part to the existence of gatekeepers.

He acted as if it was just a shake off, he would get back to his work because in the history of black Americans, we have always nullified their experiences, unlike other groups of people. That was literally an orchestrated attack against their lives for centuries.

RIGHT?

A mixture of disinfectant, soap, and floral air invaded his broad nostrils inside the neglected space, as his workmates had brought in a group of prisoners from the ongoing demonstration. His quivering arm scrolled the tap on the basin, and echoes of running water and footsteps passing the discreet door began. Justin poured drops of colorless liquid onto his parched face while exhaling. He occasionally coughed as his heart pounded.

Maybe in the events, he wanted to show them how we deserve some grace in this country, but he wasn't willing to put his life on the line. It was the underbelly of what I said, negating the fact that his workmates have been historically heinous to date toward black people.

And there were no other people on the planet being scrutinized like us.

That was an oppression disaster. Okay, and should've been treated like one. The reality lingered by putting everything on a piece of paper, of what black Americans have been through and continue to go through, it simply does not compare to anyone else's plight. There weren't other groups of people being scrutinized for not surviving heinous, unwanted, and unprovoked violent acts done to them for the better. In fact, there is always empathy toward the other group, other than the injured black Americans.

"Oh, you're simply not being tough enough." We say.

His eyes landed on the wide mirror while the fog blurred his vision. He checked his black jacket, grabbing his pills. His jaw tightened as he opened his meds, taking two other blue pills immediately and drinking tap water. Justin closed his textured mouth and gazed steadily at himself with minimal movement. Also, a knock on the door had him lean and pull away.

"Are you okay, Justin?" The Sheriff asked eventually.

He turned his drawn together brows with his hands clenching into fits.

"Yes. I am fine!" Justin opened the wooden

door, walking with her.

The air had tingled with coal smoke, within a partitioned and sterilized van where Doctor Sarah, Mel Ling, and Colton sat down, leaving the facility in Changping. The wild pine trees created a tension, and the drive became too quiet for anyone's liking. The outer districts with rows of high rises, shuttered shops, and masked pedestrians.

Her brown hands shook, and colorless moisture exuded through the pores of her glass face. Also, Mel leaned forward with an attempt to stop her, but she had no idea how to play her cards. She ground her teeth while Sarah side-eyed Colton, who looked through the window.

The industrial zones unfolded into the dense rhythm of Beijing life. Traffic was disorderly, with electric scooters, black Audis, and delivery bikes weaving through the lane as the street lights flashed in Mandarin and English. Loudspeakers announcements of a melodic lady could be heard, and also vendors selling candled hawthorn and steamed buns near the station exit.

"How long have you worked for the

facility?"

Dr. Sarah broke the awkward silence between them.

"Now seven months."

Mel Ling pursed her curved lips.

"And you were promoted to the chief research officer that fast?"

She pulled her head away in sudden disbelief with a wandering eye contact.

"I'm good at my job. Why not?" Her hands were intertwined. "And when our chief had passed away… I meant she resigned." She involuntarily paused in deliberate motion, and Sarah stepped back, maybe terrified of the smoke.

CHAPTER SEVENTEEN

The van had pulled up around eleven in the morning, the sky was bruised gray in Wuhan with a damp and metallic atmosphere, clinging to their skin like a second layer of breath. The city hums had been restrained with urgency, and motorbikes weaved through traffic.

An elderly vendor set up stalls of steamed buns and bitter tea, as the distant echo from a loudspeaker announced public health updates. The doors opened, and Dr. Mel led as they stepped out, in crisp Tyvek suits and N95 masks. Also, their ID badges swung like pendulums, yet their lined faces stayed composed and alert. Their eyes scanned the hospital's façade, noting the faded signage and the surveillance cameras tucked into corners. Mel stood upright, and her expression was unreadable. Behind her, Dr. Sarah adjusted her facial mask, and she began thumbing through a leather-bound notebook.

Dr. Mel used fluent Mandarin when she addressed a chubby woman, in her forties, and she introduced herself as Dr. Lisa Chen. Colton carried a slim tablet, its screen flickered with data pulled from satellite feeds and internal hospital logs.

They met a Chinese liaison, Dr. Zhao Wen, whose smile melted everyone down, yet his lips seemed tight and rehearsed. He bowed slightly, gesturing toward the door with a sweep of his rounded, clammy arm.

"Welcome to Wuhan Central Hospital," He said. "We are honored by your visit."

But his brown eyes blinked nervously toward the security cameras. The lobby was dimly lit, with shimmering panels overhead and a lingering scent of ethanol. It pulsed with a quiet dread. CT machines hummed relentlessly, their screens displaying lungs clouded with ground-glass opacities.

The two young nurses around the lobby moved after Dr. Sarah approached them, and her hazel eyes fell on the janitor, who paused mid-mopping, avoiding eye contact with the American doctors.

Dr. Zhao led them to the corridor that smelled of iodine and mildew. Posters of ways to prevent getting affected by COVID-19 hang on the walls past room 23, where a young doctor around twenty-two, lay in isolation, whose chart was missing in their records.

The security guard stood too close to the door marked 'Authorized Personnel Only' while the American doctors slowed, watching the patient motionless, oxygen tubes snaking across his pale face.

"This way, please." Dr. Lisa Chen insisted. "The research wing is prepared."

"Was he exposed to the wet market?" Sarah began asking hard questions, and Dr. Zhao retreated, running his brown eyes toward Mel, who pursed her lips tightly.

"No. He… he had no known exposure." The Americans exchanged glances while his raw voice came in low.

As they entered the conference room with lacquered walls, and a faint smell of stale tea. The white doctors sat across from Dr. Zhao, Mel, and Lisa, the virologist, with a shaky palm on the center round table. Also, Dr. Zhao's eyes flickered toward the door every few minutes.

Dr. Sarah opened her case. "We reviewed

your genome logs. Several entries were overwritten. And some showed deletions. Timestamps never matched at all. WHY?"

Dr. Zhao made loud noises of amusement while Americans narrowed their eyes.

"Ah, yes. That was a clerical error. Maybe our systems are outdated."

"Outdated systems don't erase metadata. Someone must've done this manually."

Colton leaned forward as his gloved fingers glitched on the slim tablet he held, as Dr. Mel shifted her quivering fingers tapping the rhythm against her thigh, and Dr. Lisa glanced at the ceiling as if her whole world had collapsed.

"We're not here to accuse anyone, but to understand the reasoning behind it."

Dr. Sarah's metallic voice wafted through the ooze, but still with lingering grief. The room became thick with unspoken gestures. Dr. Zhao began to fumble with his phone, pretending to receive a message.

"Excuse me," He said. "Urgent matter."

"I'll come with you."

Dr. Lisa Chen joined him as they stormed

out of the conference, leaving Sarah startled. Everyone could smell the terror in their veins. Also, Dr. Mel led her visitors to the side wing where they found a young cleaning lady whose footsteps weakened, and she fainted, lying unconscious while a pool of colorless liquid leaked from Mel's skull. Their eyes narrowed as Dr. Zhao approached her.

"This must be a distraction."

He raised his heavy voice, "NO, NO… Can't you see she may be…?"

"I accessed your internal logs. I know about the suppressed case files from July."

Dr. Mel pulled his head like she had been electrified, as Dr. Zhao's glass face was drained of color.

"You… you must understand. We were told to contain panic."

Mel took a few steps with a quivering hand. "To protect the public."

Her voice trembled. "We never understood how bad it was, until it happened."

The Americans pulled away as she walked closer.

"We were told it was pneumonia. Then the

deaths started."

Dr. Sarah wrinkled her nose as these colorless liquids swam from her eyes.

"But I told you about my son's death, and you never found it in your heart to show any transparency."

The air became intense, her arm ran through her pockets as she asked for a bottle of water, taking her meds while these excruciating pains heavily sat on her chest.

CHAPTER EIGHTEEN

"You're telling me he traveled with the virus here?"

Behind the locked door, in a server room smelling ozone and secrecy, Dr. Sarah found a server rack humming quietly, which Dr. Colton plugged into his slim tablet.

"Yes..." Mel tightened her jaw. "He came from Africa."

Africa is not a country, but a continent consisting of fifty-four sovereign states.

However, I have never understood why we Africans have always been the target. Have we ever committed some offense to the Western world? Because again, people from developed countries do not treat, act, or share the same sentiments, bad attitudes, and beliefs toward other developed states.

"Which airlines did he use?"

"Well---I am not sure. I will inquire about the airlines, but that's it...."

The files began to download amidst these wandering eyes and banging chests. Dr. Zhao paced around, as his brown thumb rested on his chin, thinking out loud at the exit way.

"So, why did he have to travel to Africa when China is the trading center?'

"I have no idea." Mel had involuntary pauses while she spoke.

Lung scans, suppressed case reports, encrypted emails, and internal memes marked 'Do Not Share' landed on the tablet. Dr. Mel Ling swallowed a gulp as she nodded. Among the files, records of three Wuhan institute researchers had fallen ill in early August 2019.

Dr. Zhao slumped against the exit door. "We were told to protect the public. To avoid panic."

"Shut up."

Dr. Mel rose her metallic voice while these greenish muscles displayed her face.

"No, no, you were silenced." Dr. Sarah knelt beside him while he shook beyond measure. "You were all silenced." She looked back at fuming Mel, who had crossed her arms.

The heart of Brussels wore a winter coat. Its cobblestones slack with rain, facades glistening under low-hanging clouds, and the scents of roasted chestnuts curled in the air from the vendors. The city was damp with our memories, since we had shared a cozy time in a fine mist that clung to our room windows. The gray skies muted tones and occasional burst of color from a scarf.

Jacqueline had taken me to Mont des Arts, where she stood still, her back to the city and watching the spire of the Hotel de Ville pierce the sky. Her coat was a deep oxblood, clinched at her small waist, the collar turned up against the chill. She was such a beautiful woman. Not only that, but my breath could easily be seen, and our cheeks flushed from the walk.

Her short, gloved fingers carried a small paper bag with two warm waffles, steam coming from the folds. Furthermore, she sent me these half smiles and signals that drew life out of me. I rubbed my gloved hands. Also, her fingers brushed my forearm during these tender laughs.

The most important moments in life come when we stop caring about what the world or our culture thinks about who we love. When we cut them from determining who we desire to love and immerse ourselves in their presence without influence.

My brown nut eyes saw her in many ways I never did because I had a preconceived notion of what kind of woman I was supposed to marry for mama, but now she had already gone.

"Come on."

Her golden eyes searched my face with sudden hunger like she wanted to eat me, but she passed her waffle, and I hesitated because her soft, high-pitched voice had lust and uplifted her well-knitted brows, rising her cheekbones. I watched her little face movements, and when she smiled, I leaned in, with relaxed shoulders, and I ran my arm onto her blemish-free, chiseled jaw.

She remained still while I kissed her curved lips, and her arms caressed my waist so tightly. I almost got a boner as a not-young man, and his wife saw us locking over these burning flames in a tucked-away café near Place Sainte Catherine. And their laughter came in low, the one made for strange love birds.

We walked toward the Sablon, where antique shops glittered like hearths and their scents of old wood, and forgotten stories hung in the air. I hoped we wouldn't have to forget ours. I yearned to always wake up seeing her square face and the painting of her glowing charm. She was the artist who skillfully molded every broken piece of myself back together.

And I had grown to never value my happiness ever since I lost my mama, but she gave me a sudden warmth of trusting life once again. I held her up onto my broad shoulders like a painting, and she drew her textured lips to mine. She had a citrus taste, the one that never goes away. We were under the streetlamp, and our shadows emerged.

CHAPTER NINETEEN

I dreamed of this ever since I was a child, to have someone who saw me for who I am, not what they perceived me to be. Because if we're being honest, my perception was already dictated before even my birth by the world's gatekeepers on whom and what I deserved.

Meeting her was surreal, and I struggled both mentally and emotionally; however, her divine presence still brought some flames inside me. I am a man who takes things on face or surface value, but as for my blackness, I couldn't risk having her, no matter how bad I wanted to.

Yet I believed her.

We had been together for a few days, but we were starving and building our relationship, which challenged certain norms and bonded us solely through love. But this wasn't a kumbaya project, and I still acknowledged the lines we cut in our tribes for the sake of our protection.

However, in case we don't, I believe we're strong, we can come together, regroup, and recollect ourselves and culture because we're such a diverse family, and should trust one another. Even if I seemed constantly reminded of why I shouldn't be with her. I was in a state of paranoia, running numbers, reading the signs, and going nuts.

Jacqueline had driven me insane, and in real life, you can't win like that; you've got to trust your gut regardless of the unsettling circumstances. Because if you can't ever differentiate any, you're gone. And for me, maybe I needed her to calm that scared black boy inside me from Otodo-Gbame, who never dreamt of meeting someone like her.

Pretty Chioma made me see, but Jacqueline calmed me down, which scarred the shit out of me, and also added sprinkling fire wax within my bones. The excitement, but also my horrendous reality as a black man in America, lingered inside my head.

While my heart pounded through my frail walls because I could be *George Floyd on that summit.* My story would be *rewritten on what occurred for me,* and *the lies* could become *my TRUTH* because if we're being honest, there's always a little doubt in people's minds about my integrity, and we all know people might not believe mine.

Our table had been tucked in the corner, half-shaded by a vine-covered trellis, and also a flickering candle between us since the sun had not quite set. She was wrapped inside my jacket since her oxblood coat, only clinched at her small waist, and she had curled up with mint tea while I nursed on trappist beer.

Our laughter softened, she watched the horizon, the sky was a watercolor washed by apricot and lavender, and then she turned, "I never expected to feel like this." My shaky palm reached out, brushing her cotton-like wrist. My goodness, she was a very beautiful woman. "Me neither."

The whites in her eyes made us pause long enough for the atmosphere to shift, and she leaned forward with her small elbows on the rounded table. She told me about her last relationship with a man named Jason Diederik, whom she relentlessly loved five years ago. She used to work here, and this man brought a new lady as the jazz playlist hummed beneath their cutlery.

The brutal part, she was the waiting staff who watched in quiet precision, dressed in a crisp white shirt and black apron.

"He treated me horrendously; maybe I loved him too much."

She pointed to the bench where she once sat, crying into a paper cone of frites.

"You're not too much for me," she looked into my nut eyes in search of the truth.

"You'll never be," I promised her, and she nodded while our wet eyes glistened.

Our Captain entered his house like a thief, his coat folded over his arm, his shirt slightly rumpled, and his breath carried a faint scent of red wine and someone else's scent as he closed the door softly, almost reverently, like the quietness might erase what he had done.

The hallway dimmed with their son's jacket hung crookedly on the hook. Also, a school drawing---crayon scribbles of a family fluttered from the fridge in the pale kitchen. He paused, listening to the sound of surgical rhythm, from a knife against wood.

Clinton tightened his jaw when his eyes landed on her slicing collard greens. Her movements were deliberate, almost ceremonial, as she wore a faded apron over a pale blouse, and her long sleeves were rolled up. The kitchen smelled of garlic, thyme, and some buns burning faintly in the oven.

Their son sat on the floor nearby, building a tower with plastic blocks, humming to himself, and occasionally glancing up at his mother.

"Smells good." He stepped into the kitchen, loosening his tie, but she never turned since her fingers continued with the knife rhythm.

He moved closer, placing his keys on the counter. "Long day," he offered, and she turned slowly, her wet eyes meeting his with no rage, but just a quiet, devastating layer full of numbness.

"Was she enough to forget who you are?" Her voice was low, steady.

"What's that supposed to mean?" He stiffened.

Her snowy hands wiped on a towel, and then she folded it neatly.

"I know who she is, what you said to her, and how you even said it."

"You're being dramatic."

"For everything I've done for you? You think Am Theater or a joke?"

"Please… just calm down." He begged.

"No, no, you don't ever calm me down, it's been fifteen years of this marriage. You're such an ingrate soul."

"It was a mistake. It didn't mean anything."

She made a dry, loud, sharp laughter coming from her excruciating pain.

"You've always rehearsed that line, didn't you? You must've practiced it in her bathroom mirror while she was still healing from your loads?"

His hands folded, creasing his forehead.

"Mama, is dinner ready?"

Their son looked up, and she knelt beside him, brushing his silver white hair back.

"Almost, sweetheart. Go wash your hands upstairs."

He ran off, and the relentless silence sapped everyone's energy.

"You brought her into our lives, didn't you?" She stood, facing her husband again.

His overly laced shoes stepped forward, voice rising. "You're twisting this." He struck her cheek hard, thundering the entire household, but she didn't flinch, and her hands held onto her reddish face.

"Now, I am seeing the real you."

He reached for her arm, and she stepped back as colorless liquid swam out of her eyes. "Don't you dare touch me?" She turned to the counter and picked up the knife again, out of security.

"I didn't mean to hurt you."

The air thickened while the pot on the stove began to boil over, unnoticed. Also, outside, the tram passed again, and rumbled a distant echo of tension inside.

"If you think I'll leave you with our son, think again!" He made empty threats.

CHAPTER TWENTY

This man reminded me of a lawyer. He was so good with his words. Dr. Zhang talked circles around the Americans, but, at that point Dr. Sarah knew she could shift his game in their favor. She had never changed her mind on interviewing the man they all 'claimed' came from Africa. Dr. Mel Ling folded like a ton of bricks; that woman literally never had any backbone.

None.

Both of these doctors seemed ready to turn on each other, which was fine because they were two snakes keeping relevant sequences on today's situation. And they could never trust them again. First, they were going behind each other's backs and telling secrets to her.

They had one-on-one, outside the data room.

"You played me." She ran her gloved hands on the surgical cap wrapped around her black hair in disbelief.

"I didn't play you. I'm only loyal to China."

"So you lied to me?"

"I lied to you because you broke my trust."

He clenched his brown teeth, lowering his tone. "You brought Americans to my door."

She pursed her lips. "How many times have you lied to me?"

"I've lied to you a lot." He raised his brows while he looked around the door.

"Okay." She lowered her tone while this colorless liquid swam in her eyes. He ran his plumpy arm to reach her, but she took a few steps back.

"I think… I made a bad choice, and I do regret it." He tightened his rounded jaw.

"And I blew up our operations, in a person I shouldn't have put my trust in."

She ended up laughing out with severe envy.

"You're only scared of the Vice Minister."

"Because you've always gotten off scot-free, unlike us."

"Come on." She darted her eyes.

"No, all you have to do is get your back blown from this as far as I can tell."

He slouched his quivering shoulders close to the white walls.

"That's so crazy."

"No, no, don't make fickle. I've loved you

for so long, and you were with him all along, a married man."

"They're heading to the isolation suite."

Dr. Lisa interrupted, and they walked hurriedly to join them. The room was sealed behind two layers of reinforced glass, with a narrow vestibule between them where air was filtered and sterilized. A red light above the inner door pulsed, signaling bio-hazard containment. As they walked inside, the air was unnaturally still, pressured to prevent any particles from escaping.

The matte white walls looked theatrical, like a set designed to evoke clinical dread. Also, a single surveillance camera blinked in the corner, and its lens trained on the patient's every twitch.

The man lay on a gurney, slightly reclined, and his dry brown skin glistened with a faint sheen of sweat. He was shirtless beneath a thin white hospital sheet, revealing electrodes taped across his hairy chest, and their wires snaked toward a monitor that displayed erratic vitals: elevated heart rate, and fluctuating oxygen saturation.

A nasal cannula fed him oxygen, even though his breathing appeared to steady, also his brown eyes darted between the two American doctors behind the glass, and Dr. Zhang stood beside him with a clipboard in his quivering hand.

A portable ventilator hummed quietly at his side, not in use but present like a prop in a courtroom drama. An IV bag hung from a steel pole, dripping saline into his arm, though the tubing was kinked as if left out on purpose. Beside the bed, a laptop displayed a spreadsheet of travel data: flight numbers, timestamps, and layovers. Dr. Mel gestured using her hand, narrating the patient's journey from Kinshasa to Addis Ababa, then to Guangzhou.

"He used Ethiopian Airlines."

She pointed as if the name itself carried viral weight.

"Did you feel symptoms before or after the transfer in Ethiopia?" Dr. Sarah asked.

He hesitated.

"After?" She insisted.

And he nodded.

Dr. Colton shared glances with Dr. Sarah; he scribbled notes while she watched the patient's pupils dilate under the fluorescent lights.

"He was in a rural clinic in the DRC. No PPE or screening." Dr. Mel did her big one to convince her.

"He arrived here febrile, coughing blood."

The patient coughed on cue, a dry rasp that echoed in the sealed room.

When I lived in San Francisco, I was unusually fast with women. The idea of love was never on the cards for me. Maybe because I needed to find the solid woman who comforted me regardless of any life challenges. And Jacqueline did more than that; she made me a complete man. I never used to feel like a lion in the jungle; moreover, in my tribe, I was always on the losing side.

My mama, and so many things I had lost.

Not that they could be replaceable.

None of them could ever be…

But she made Goliath out of me, dominating her, and I blew us from our situations in the past. We stepped out of the restaurant into the crisp autumn air, and her arm had looped through mine. The sun shifted slightly, casting longer shadows across the cobblestones. The street was alive but rushed, also cyclists glided past. This man, who was a musician, played a slow, melancholic tune on a violin near the corner as we headed toward the Marolles district, winding through narrow alleys lined with antique shops and faded murals.

She paused at a storefront displaying vintage postcards and porcelain figurines, her gloved fingers trailed the glass as my brown eyes watched her with amusement. I gently tugged her hand, leading her forward like I even knew where we were going.

As we passed the bakery, the scent of fresh bread and cinnamon rolls spilled into the street. She insisted we stop for a pain au chocolat, and we shared it on a bench in Place du Jeu de Balle, where the flea market wound down. Around us, vendors packed up crates of old books, brass candlesticks, and sepia-toned photographs.

Also, a ten-year-old boy chased a blue balloon, and an old man fed pigeons from a paper bag.

"The day we met, I was terrified of you." She twitched her fingers against my thighs.

"I don't know what changed, but I can be myself around you." She leaned against my broad shoulder, and my inside shifted with a kind of quiet alertness, not cold or warm, just relaxation.

"And I never used to feel like a woman, but you, Mr. Ahmed Olaoluwatomijogun, make love feel real, but not fairytale."

Her eyes flickered every time I shifted, and her quivering arms had crisscrossed.

"I... I want to be with you, Ms. Jacqueline De Vrles." I inhaled sharply, then spoke fast. "Not just on good days. I want the cloudy evenings, the fights about laundry, and the weird silences. I want it all with you."

She pulled away from me as her gloves squeezed her wet eyes in disbelief.

"Are you proposing to me?"

She stood, distancing herself, and her hands covered her masked face. I heard soft laughs from her, and I almost sobbed. Mama would've been the happiest woman if she had ever lived to witness this day.

"Yes… Will you marry me?"

She reached out, her soft hands brushing my wrist.

"Yes." She accepted.

CHAPTER TWENTY-ONE

Owls don't owe the same disposition toward white people; they hold onto us, no, they don't. That doesn't exclude the anti-black people among our communities who hate their blackness and, on top of that, carry this ridiculous prejudice. These black people are already predisposed toward black Americans who lean anti-black.

Why is that?

The double standards and hypocrisy.

I hate to acknowledge this, but it is what it is.

The owl worship and supremacy? Their default understanding of the gatekeepers, regardless of what they have done, are innocent. Versus how they viewed what the black Americans have passed through as offensive. The sickening attempt to inflame their offenses for what it was.

Yes, some groups of black people were and are anti-black.

The reality was that if you take the black people out of the equation, you can find the same groups doing it to themselves, the othering of their own people based on tribe, background, language, states, and all these minor things.

Right?

TO THEIR *OWN* CHILDREN, mind you, popped out of their womb.

Their bloodline and DNA straight from the well.

Justin's uniform had already become heavier than Kevlar beneath, and loud voices inside his head grew larger than before, tightening his chest during the evenings, and whispering questions and doubts into his ears if any of this was even worth the price of his own people.

During the traffic stops, curling around his spine whenever he walked into rooms, having some owl officers who spoke in clipped tones and shared glances they never intended for him to understand. In the tree-lined street, protestors had gathered again, placards raised, 'White silence gives consent to violence.' 'We cannot die in silence,' a white woman with blue eyes held these cards amongst other people of color who walked, chanting rhythmically but restrained.

He had been two blocks away, monitoring the crowd flow, and trying to breathe through the familiar tightness in his throat. The vivid images inside tormented him, his fingers pulled out his meds, and he took two pills without water. He stayed in the car for a minute, calming himself down.

Then he heard it. Not the chants, but the rupture.

Screams. Not slogans.

Justin opened the car door, for the first time, jogging toward the sound, heart hammering, and colorless liquid blooming beneath his white vest. The same officers he watched in the cell. Sergeant Klein, who wished to have been allowed to teach the black jailed prisoners a lesson, and his companion, Officer Dorsey, struck a lady to the ground.

Her braids covered the reddish residue on her coffee face. Also, her arms shielded her head from their laced boots. This teenager streamed a bloody birth from her full lips, and the crowd backed away, hands raised and pleading for mercy.

It wasn't just chaos but cruelty.

Justin froze.

And he had to choose either his job or humanity.

His gut called him to run as he had always done.

He stepped forward.

"STOP!" His firm voice shook. "They're not resisting."

Klein turned first, narrowing his hazel eyes. "Back off, Justin."

"You don't give orders here." Officer Dorsey kicked in with a parched forehead.

"I'm not giving orders," the ground beneath his boots trembled. "I'm stopping an assault."

Sergeant Klein shoved him hard. "You want to be one of them so bad."

Dorsey raised and struck his baton to his ribs, and Klein punched his sharp jaw. A not-young man was shoved to the ground as well. Also, a boy in the hoodie took a blow to his stomach, and he crumpled. The crowd gasped, recoiled, and tried to help shield one another.

"You want to be a hero so bad?"

Another baton came for him. Not from the 'threatening crowd', and he had a sharp crack to his shoulder. He folded his body, knees buckling, and tried to communicate, but their blows, from hatred, kept on coming.

Fists.

Boots.

Justin clenched his teeth, stained with fresh reddish liquid as his own brothers in navy blue turned on him like he was a threat. The demonstrators screamed as he hit his head onto the pavement, and his vision blurred. The concrete bit into his cheek while some people filmed and cried. The teenager's hand trembled as she reached for his bleeding face.

And maybe Justin's anxiety always protected him. He heard this voice whispering into his ear again.

'You've never been safe.'

'Not really.'

'Not ever.'

Maybe he hoped to bridge the gap between police and our own people, but these gatekeepers hated us.

For simply breathing.

These owls were too hungry to get rid of us.
For simply existing.

CHAPTER TWENTY-TWO

When I was young, around three years old. Mama used to leave me at Uncle Toriola's place early in the morning to get her fruits and veggies to the Balogun market. But then he used to wake and make me do pull-ups. Also, he would tell me to run up a mountain, race hard like my life depends on it, and never give up or get lost.

Because it never mattered if I ran more than three times for the foundation of strength, because truly life is the hardest thing we all do, and humans must be the strongest creatures after all.

It took more than perseverance since we were little.

Some gave up along the way.

Others didn't even make it.

It's so hard being alive.

And we wonder who we serve or our purpose.

Our Captain's wife stood at the threshold of their son's room in despair, her hand resting on the doorframe as if she reflected on what he had done. The house had a sudden quietness that sack life out of them. Also, no cartoons hummed on his small tablet, or the thudding of his small feet.

Just a low, rhythmic wheeze of their son's breathing.

The dim room lit by the soft blue glow of the nightlight shaped like a whale. His bed was a tangle of sheets and a stuffed rabbit. Also, the one-eyed bear he refused to hold. However, he lay curled on one side, his knees drawn up, and his body slack with colorless liquid. His silver white hair clung to his forehead, and his small lips were almost parted and dry.

Not only that, but a cough rattled through him, wet and deep, like something to claw its way out. She crossed the room, barefoot, her white cardigan slipping off one shoulder as she knelt pressing into the wooden floor. Her fingers brushed their son's cheek, burning hot, and his eyes fluttered open, and unfocused.

"Mama, it hurts."

She swallowed. "It's okay, baby."

We all had seen the rising cases, and the pediatric ward at Saint-Pierre overflowed. But this was her child, mothers can do anything, even if sacrificing their own lives to save their sons. They always do. My mama saved me her whole life, and I would never have been anything or even survived without her. She was me, and I was her.

She pressed the thermometer to his temple, and the temperature was 39.8 °C. She knew while her shaking arms wrapped him in his star-patterned blanket, the one he used to call his 'lucky charm.'

He whimpered as she lifted him, his limbs limped and his breath became shallow, hitting hard her rounded neck while they went through a narrow stair, past the framed family portraits. Her hazel eyes looked around, and she couldn't get a sight of him.

The supposed patient at Wuhan hospital, Mr. Liang, had gone missing around three in the evening from room number 203. But before he did, there was a brief blackout. When the feed resumed, none of the American doctors could be seen by Dr. Mel Ling and Zhang. And their hearts hammered as Mel stormed out of the restricted room into the control.

She pulled her hair into a tight bun, with a parched forehead, and also her gloved fingers scanned the footage---two figures in white coats, one short, the other stocky, moving swiftly down the corridor with the patient slumped between them.

"SEAL THE EXISTS." She raised her heavy voice at Dr. Zhang.

"Notify your Ministry. No one leaves without clearance."

"Let's go."

He called Dr. Lisa Chen while they dispersed, and guards were stationed at every stairwell and elevator. The hospital's underground parking was secured. Mel moved through the halls like a blade as the colorless liquid dripped down her spine, cutting through protocol as her personal phone vibrated. She experienced intense chest tightness and realized he had gone behind her back, confessing to doing so anyway.

"You have twelve hours." She tensed her jaws. "If they reach the consulate, you're compromised, but **PRAY** they don't cross the river, or else you'll be expendable."

No name or pleasantries.

Just the weight of the state pressing against her back.

And her mouth went dry as she tightened her throat.

She didn't say a word, but her hand trembled like an earthquake, and she clenched it into a fist, thus lowering her phone. This cold flushed spread across her chest, and her knees felt hollow. Also, her breath came in short, clipped bursts as she leaned on the concrete, grounding herself.

"Understood."

She stormed into the operation center, her voice had been stripped away.

"Full lockdown. No exists or elevators exist. I want thermal scans of every duct. Every shaft. They're still inside."

Updates came in from Dr. Zhang.

A nurse reported seeing two white foreigners near the incinerator chute, with no cameras or guards. Additionally, he claimed that their sick janitor had confessed to disabling the surveillance grid for five minutes. She would be paid since the discarded oxygen mask had been found where she kept her cleaning equipment.

Dr. Mel's mind raced while she walked with two guards to the old maternity wing; maybe she thought Americans needed to isolate so they could come up with a plan. She descended into the subbasement herself with no guards or entourage. Just the hum of machinery and the smell of rust and antiseptic. She passed the old autopsy room, with the disused laundry tunnel.

CHAPTER TWENTY-THREE

Dr. Zhang was the oldest among the staff of the hospital, and Mel believed he wanted to prove himself to the Ministry. Like he can he do better than her or the rest of them? He seemed like he was helping out, but not really assisting her. However, the parched lines on her forehead were visible, yet she let him feel like he was in charge, maybe for the bigger picture.

"I'm going to kill her."

Mel was willing to commit to whatever she had to do to get to the end of the road alive.

No matter what!

And Zhang gave orders:

Like, go check the old maternity wing.

If you thought so, keep going and don't ever stop.

Call me every ten minutes.

You see, now you're learning.

You have to be stronger than us.

"Yeah, no problem, no problem, no problem." She said.

However, in Mel's mind. "SHUT THE HELL UP." But she couldn't risk saying it to his face during this situation when she felt she was not in a position of power on the State's board.

Mel would rather prove them wrong and change their perception as a woman who claimed to have made it on favoritism and sleeping around with the Vice Minister. So, Mel had a plan in the works to prove she was more than just an accessory or image.

She had ordered a sweep of the hospital's used wings, old surgical theaters, the west wing maternity ward, and storage rooms. Her mind raced through possibilities, the nurse who reported seeing the two Americans near a radiology lab, and she sent two guards with her. The corridor smelled of dust and iodine; however, she found a trail of discarded gloves, a broken vial, and a footprint in spilled saline.

She paused outside, and her quivering arms rested around her waist. The muffled voices came from the inside, and Mel signaled in silence, and her team burst in. Their textured lips opened in the N95 masks since the room was empty but recently used. The oxygen tanks still hissed; a tablet of lithium left behind showed the presence of Dr. Sarah. Also, the window was ajar, leading to the alley behind the hospital. She stilled in one position, tightening her jaws.

2:57 PM--- The Quiet before.

The hospital hummed with its usual nocturnal routine, the soft beep of the monitor and the low murmur of the nurses at the station. Dr. Mel, in a loose bun, hunched over a slim Tablet, Colton handed her to review the data vitals. Downstairs, in the corridor of maintenance, Dr. Zhang stood beside a fuse box, and his white coat folded over his not youthful arm like a waiter's towel.

He checked his small watch at about three in the evening while he received a text.

"Now"

The lights died with a soft click, then silence and a breathless pause. Emergency lights flickered on in red and amber. Downstairs in the hall, a chubby nurse gasped, a monitor flatlined for a moment before rebooting.

"What the hell...?" Mel opened her textured lips.

In the dark, two figures in surgical masks

and black windbreakers moved swiftly. Dr. Sarah and Colton wheeled a gurney down the side of the corridor, bypassing the main elevators. The supposed patient still lay on the bed when Zhang stood, holding the door open. No words, but he just nodded while the patient met them at the old maintenance stairwell.

While Dr. Mel rushed to the patient's bed, her brown eyes widened since it was

Empty, and as she turned, the doctor bumped into both Dr. Zhang and Lisa Chen.

Around 3:12 pm, the sickly janitor was mopping near the west wing's electrical panel. Also, she wore headphones, listening to a scratchy Mandopop, as Dr. Zhang slipped a small screwdriver into the panel's lock and left it ajar. He then directed the guard a few minutes later.

"You were near the panel?"

"What?" She removed the headphones.

"Come with us."

Dr. Zhang opened a secure chat on his slim tablet after he gave orders to Dr. Mel to check the old maternity wing.

"She's running insane."

"Really?"

Dr. Sarah couldn't help herself.

"Ha-ha… The janitor is now in custody."

"We're now in position."

Dr. Colton joined their group chat.

"You've got six minutes."

"Don't worry, you'll have your seat."

"Thank you, man." He tightened his *rounded jaw. "Windows prepped."*

Zhang closed the tablet as he watched his reflection on the dark screen.

He then smirked. "I want her out so bad."

Inside the pediatric COVID ward. The air smelled faintly disinfectant and latex while rain streaked the window in slow, uneven lines. The room was dim, just with a soft glow of the monitor beside the five-year-old, and also the occasional beep of oxygen saturation alerts.

The Captain's wife sat in the corner chair, knees pulled to her chest, arms wrapped around her like a child. Her eyes were swollen as she turned toward the window, but unfocused since she had been crying for hours.

"He wouldn't be here if you hadn't." Her low, heavy voice cracked.

Captain Clinton stood near the sink, clenching his rugged hands, but failed to say a word. Maybe since he knew she was right. He had broken the quarantine rules, and he lied about where he had gone. And now this situation might cost him their son.

"You brought it into our house… into his lungs."

She sobbed again, and her body folded forward as if the grief had crushed her. Also, her quivering fingers dug into her scalp. Clinton stepped forward, but she raised her voice.

"Don't. Don't dare touch me."

CHAPTER TWENTY-FOUR

I hate projecting my paranoia onto others, but as a Black man, I have no choice. Jacqueline and I felt like the impossible had happened. I was a very reserved man. And building trust with her? I was so proud of myself because it used to be hard for me to come out of my shell, even a little. My insecurities also came to the forefront, as a thirty-three-year-old man with no family.

Being myself and having her accept me was such a freeing experience, and I hoped to love, cherish, and protect her. Regardless of any unfortunate circumstances. I had never imagined being loved by her. So, obviously, I wasn't good at picking on social cues.

Her black boots scraped the gravel, and her coat flared in the wind. The mask clung to her mouth while everyone's eyes stilled on her. She failed to give any contact information to the mourners. Not even to her mother, who stood rigid near the priest, nor to the other family members in attendance. She walked straight to the shimmering coffin.

Dark wood, gold trim, a velvet lining glimpsed through the glass.

It looked too good for my liking, and called for royalty.

Not for someone who once walked barefoot in Otodo-Gbame.

Or worked as a retailer in the House of H & Z.

And also proposed without a ring.

Jacqueline collapsed onto the coffin. Not gently, and her body folded like a broken hinge. Furthermore, her fingers clawed the polished surface, leaving streaks of fog and sweat. Also, her used to be ladylike sobs had turned into an animal, super wet, guttural, and uncontainable. Her mask slipped off completely as her mother flinched.

Not at the grief, but at the spectacle since she felt her daughter was embarrassing her in front of everyone. Also, her cousin, Coen, was filming discreetly and ready to go viral on TikTok. The priest in a stole cleared his throat as he spoke of resurrection.

Jacqueline's cheeks streaked with colorless liquid and snot.

On the first floor, in the unused radiology lab, the window was already unlatched. Rain tapped against the glass like impatient fingers. Dr. Colton lifted the patient first through, then Dr. Sarah climbed out, her gloved fingers slipped slightly on the wet sill, but Colton held as she passed through.

"You better hold up." Zhang texted while the entire crew was outside the room.

Dr. Mel Ling burst into the room seconds too late. Even though the door was still open, cold air rushed inside, carrying a scent of wet concrete and diesel. She leaned out, scanning the alley below.

She saw nothing.

Apart from the sound of a distant engine and the echo of her breath.

The monitor beeped, and a chubby nurse walked inside the Pilot's son's room to check the IV. She left without a word, and the silence hit them harder than before.

"I... I had no idea..."

"You didn't care." She cut him off. "That's the truth. You never cared, right?"

"Helena?" He parched his forehead.

As she stood, walking to their son's bedside, she stroked his silver white hair gently. Her tears fell onto the blanket. He was behind her, but she never once turned.

"You're not serious." His voice was low, but the panic made it brittle.

"You're horrible---I hate you so much."

He laughed, but it cracked halfway through.

"I… I think I'm divorcing you."

"Now? You want to do this now?" He pulled his face away, trying to make her feel terrible about herself. "Our son is in the ICU. You're such a bad mother."

She turned, and her eyes were bloodshot.

"You're right. Our son is alone." He swallowed while she agreed with him.

"I've always been alone while you were with her. Right?"

He stepped forward. "It's not what you think."

She threw her right sandal, and he bent, hitting the wall.

"Don't dare call me crazy."

He grabbed her small wrist. "You think you're stronger than me? Or even be able to survive without me?"

She yanked free. "I already have."

These sudden colorless liquids swam in his eyes like she had betrayed his trust.

"I'll change. I swear. I had already ended things with her."

"You'll what?" She rolled her swollen eyes. "My trust is like a glass, once broken, it can never be mended."

He slammed his fist close to her face, just on the white wall, in extreme anger.

"You're not leaving me."

CHAPTER TWENTY-FIVE

February 5th, 2020

Sometimes we Africans tend to downplay how significant colorism is at home. The room dimmed, and the autumn light faded into a bruised amber. A mug of rooibos tea sat untouched on the windowsill, its steam curling like a burning question. A new set of shirts was folded and refolded, trousers laid out like offerings, and a small jar of makeup rested open like a confession.

I come from Nigeria, where every complexion exists; however, people with a lighter shade are prized being very brown. And please don't get me wrong, they didn't do it on purpose. That's the way we were raised. And these silly undercooked comments like, 'oh, you know, don't get out in the sun for *too long*. You're going to get too dark.'

Having lighter skin was seen as a plague of gold.

Or even being better than the rest.

I stood shirtless, my skin used to be darker skin with unyielding brown-deep mahogany undertones of copper, also my sheepish hair twisted and pulled back into a silk band.

I was barefoot, and my toes curled against the parquet floor as I watched her in a cream blouse, navy trousers, and gold studs in her ears. She had pinned her brunette hair, but a few strands escaped, curling at her temples.

"It's not about looking lighter." She held the jar in both hands. "It's about looking less."

"Less of what?"

In fact, at school, kids who were close or predominantly white were seen as more attractive than us. And also used to receive certain privileges like keeping their hair, or even never being punished like the rest. So, as teenagers with a darker complexion who wanted to fit in such a place, there was an invisible pressure we all never wanted to acknowledge that exists.

Maybe we ignored the voices in our heads, 'oh, my skin tone is just like this much off from being light enough to be cute. Or my sheepish hair is not straight enough to be allowed at school.' And I realized many people of color, not just in African states, go through colorism.

She failed to answer while her fingers dipped the sponge into the jar, with honey beige, and dabbed it gently along my angular jawline. The powder was fine, almost invisible, but changed my complexion. It dulled the glow of my skin, softened the contrast between my cheekbones and the shadows beneath them.

"When I was ten... I tanned on our Cape Town family holiday."

Jacqueline took a deep breath. "My mom said my skin looked 'angry' like she had a certain resentment."

"And you think this will make me look... more likeable?"

She flinched, but I never moved, and her arms reached for a new shirt, ivory linen, with a Mandarin collar, no buttons visible, as if it whispered cultured without saying 'African.'

But why is there a seeded hatred for darker skin and more indigenous features?

Because our skins are and were part of human nature, some people are going to be different, and seeing a whole group of people who view us as lesser than them was heart-wrenching.

"Good, no prints of the foundation." She tightened her jaw, buttoning the shirt on me. However, everything looked like a protest of who I am. She laid out the trousers, charcoal wool, tailored with a slight sheen, and Jacqueline insisted on no jewelry and also placed a pair of oxblood leather loafers beside me.

No, I had never dressed like this before; everything seemed a performativity since Jacqueline never once dressed like that, at least the few days I had been with her.

I blame it on colonization because why are we bleaching our dark skin? There are so many layers to colorism that we want to accept. Sometimes, based on our survival, like it affects our auditions or job interviews, because they may be in need of a certain complexion or hair curls. Perhaps we were too dark that our partners requested we wear a 4C texture before they introduced us to their owl parents or at work.

"My father thinks sneakers and boots are for delivery boys."

She said while I stood in front of the mirror,

and the powder had settled. The shirt fitted, and the shoes gleamed. I looked like someone else, and maybe they could call or mistake me a 'diplomat.'

"My parents won't see your kindness or cultural value, but your skin first." She touched my face while colorless liquid swam in her hazel eyes. "I want them to accept you so bad."

It hindered interracial love; certain things considered too black were not allowed on their table. So, at home, some people didn't even want to put on lotion; they only blenched so they may 'elevate their status and be put in a better position.' And sadly, it became the set standard, inspiring young dark-skinned girls to change the color of their skin.

Dr. Mel stood alone. Her coat buttoned to the throat, but her sleeves rolled up, revealing her brown forearms with dried antiseptic. Her posture was upright, but her feet angled slightly inward, and her hands collapsed behind her back. Fingers dug into each other while two officers stepped out of an elevator.

Colonel Wei, broad-shouldered, late fifties, and his face carved with decades of command.

Captain Xian was younger, wiry, and with a face like a blade. His eyes scanned the corridor where Mel stood like a sniper while they walked toward her with their laced boots.

"You were supposed to have them in your care." Colonel seemed to have lost his cool.

"I don't know where they went."

Captain Xian stepped forward with a red-blue temper.

"You do. Or you will."

"No, no, I didn't help them."

One of his hands grabbed and twisted her wrist.

"You're lying." He looked into her narrowed eyes. "Or useless."

"I never helped them escape."

"Then you are incompetent. And incompetence means treason."

He pressed two fingers beneath her jaw, just under her ear, and her knees dropped onto the ground as she ground her teeth. She landed on her hip, shaking while Captain Xian crouched beside her.

"You'll bring us results. Names. Routes. Or we will take you apart. Inch by inch."

She made loud wails while the nurses near the lobby looked back in terror.

CHAPTER TWENTY-SIX

In terms of the working ethic, I would give Dr. Mel Ling a 'B.' But in performance, a solid 'D-minus.' She needed to fish the Americans wherever they had gone, though she seemed more snorkeling than fishing, and the Chinese board had lost trust in her.

Because I worked primarily with women of color in the house of H & Z. They are the strongest, independent women I have ever gotten a chance to meet. And I think I saw it in Mel, as well as Dr. Sarah. And my greatest role model was and has always been my deceased mama.

She was the strongest woman I knew.

She moved to Otodo-Gbame immediately after my grandparents disowned her, leaving her entire family at *a teen* age, pregnant with me. So, she made an act of slaughtering for my existence. That was the main reason why I even wore a 4C texture to meet Jacqueline's parents. It was my duty to fulfill her dreams of having a happy family, and also to give back to every strong, independent woman.

Because most women a stuck in a cycle of pain that also teaches them to be kinder and more generous than men.

Most women are better than men.

Colonel Wei and Captain Xian had gone too far into the open water.

And Mel gasped, stiffening her body, and her knees buckled slightly.

"You think your degrees matter? Or they will protect you?"

Captain Xian slammed her against the wall. Her head hit the tiles, unraveling her bun from the surgical cap, and her hair spilled across her reddish face. Her shoulder then crunched against the corner of the metal cabinet. She pulled her hands, palms open in surrender.

"No one will care to ask where the doctor went."

Colonel Wei leaned in, whispering against her ear.

We glided through a modest car, rolling past manicured hedges and wrought-iron gates in Ixelles, deeper into the enclave of wealth. Their mansion was a pale limestone, with tall windows and a façade that screamed 'old money.' I had a massive beating inside the layers of my chest, and she reached for my hand before we stepped out of the car.

Her grip was firm and protective, like we had gone into a wild zone. Also, their door opened before we even rang the bell, and her mother stood in a silk blouse. Her citrus perfume was sharp, and her cheekbones never reached her eyes as she smiled at me.

"Oh." Her blue eyes paused on me. "You must be the young man."

She never cared to know my name.

"You're… very good looking. More in a bronze light side."

I have been called so many names, but I'd never once heard anyone call me that.

Perhaps because the world is so forgiving to the light-skinned, but not to us.

We get punished for our darker features every day. Her father emerged behind her wearing a blazer over a pale pink shirt, the kind of pink that whispers old money, and his handshake was firm. However, his eyes lingered too long, cataloguing and assessing me.

"Strong build," he said. "You must be working out. Or is it just… good genes?"

I stretched the corners of my full lips, exposing my teeth. "Bit of both."

"Ah," her father, with salt and pepper hair, chuckled, but it didn't reach his eyes.

"That's good."

We were ushered in, and the foyer was a cathedral-like space with a chandelier that dripped crystal like frozen tears. A staircase curved upward, the walls bore portraits of their ancestors, and some art leaning toward a colonial sepia-toned map, and oil art of men in epaulettes. The air smelled of lavender and polish in the sitting room; everything was white, the couches, orchids, and also silence.

"So," her mother handed me a glass of wine. "Tell us about your family. Like… what they do?"

I swallowed hard when I recalled my mama. "Mama passed away, but she was a local market vendor."

"Oh," her eyebrows lifted. "I'm so sorry about your mother."

"It's okay." I believed she never meant any

harm, anyway.

Her father leaned forward. "And where are you coming from?"

"San Francisco."

Jacqueline sipped on her glass with grinding teeth.

"No, I mean… before that. Your heritage?"

"Yoruba from Nigeria."

"Ah," his undertones worried me. "Well, you carry yourself with… dignity."

Jacqueline stiffened beside me while I smiled.

Dinner was served in the formal dining room, where their table stretched like a runway with a set of bone china and silverware that gleamed like surgical tools. Her father carved the roast with theatrical precision. Also, her mother had chosen the menu: roasted duck, asparagus spears, and a beet salad that bled color onto porcelain.

Her father poured wine as her mother asked. "You like spicy food?"

I swallowed.

"I hear that's popular in your culture."

"My culture?"

I tightened my jaw, drawing everyone's eye.

"You know," she insisted, waving vaguely. "Plantains. Pili-pili."

"Mama." Jacqueline dropped her fork.

"What?" She said, all innocent. "I'm trying to create a conversation."

Her father cleared his throat. "So, what do your parents do?"

I ended up smiling, but he seemed serious. "My mother was a local market vendor. And she passed away."

We all paused for a minute while the skies had gone dark.

"Oh, sorry."

CHAPTER TWENTY-SEVEN

Jacqueline, her parents, and I had stood on the back patio while her mama offered us coffee in porcelain cups.

"We're very open-minded," she cleared her throat. "We raised our daughter to see past color.

There are many things I might consider. For example, your credit score and your efforts to join certain communities. There has always been a limit, such as a business that can only succeed through networking. People with a monopoly or owl mindset tend to gatekeep certain things, like their genes, especially if a small business wants to get a loan or maybe marry their daughter.

"That's awesome." I nodded.

She smiled since I missed the irony in her voice while her arms crossed.

"We just want her to be with someone who shares her values."

We all paused as the wind rustled the hydrangeas through the window, and their black dog barked once and stopped.

It would be difficult with more hurdles to jump over to convince them. I wish they would look at my heart and hard-working qualities instead of the color of my skin, because physicality fades with time and doesn't necessarily determine success.

"She does." I tightened my jaw while I leaned close to Jacqueline.

"That's why she's me."

Jacqueline still chose me. She made me feel loved....

Entertaining segregated spaces, targeting and bombing our areas of interest, or simply rejecting us based on skin color alone stigmatizes us because owl don't let us thrive the way we want to. Her mother blinked again, her smile faltering for the first time.

And I wrapped my head around who built this society.

Whose society are we living in today?

Of course, they had to design a community that benefits them.

So, if you were not planned for, then your mindset claws to be like them, rather than distancing and thinking you will get there without them. That was the reason I had a 4C texture of foundation, to only hope of getting accepted. Racism is a mind game, and they created it, so if your mind is clouded and confused, you're going to go insane.

We have to say, *'I don't have to think that way, and I can get what I want even though I might take a different and longer path to get there. But I will make it there no matter what.'* Instead of sitting there saying, 'I am black and the system is built against me.'

Because then you've accepted defeat, and you'll never be able to reach your goal. We need to turn everything around, recognize our blackness and the system they built to oppress us, but we're strong and still determined to do what it takes to get there.

Jacqueline's mom sat in a wicker chair, close to her bald husband with a potbelly, legs crossed, and a porcelain teacup resting on her knee.

"You're very articulate." Her voice was almost syrupy. "I imagine that's served you, my daughter. Especially… considering."

"Considering?" My brows raised across my

forehead in wonder.

These paintings on their walls acknowledged that for me. We know that gatekeepers or owls exist in our communities; they recognize each other, and everyone is Caucasian. I could see their great-grandfather, who may have been a grip or prop master, going all the way back to the 1920s.

She tilted her head, the smile sharpening. "Well, you came so far. From---where was it again? Nigeria? It must've been quite the adjustment. All this civility, all the expectations."

"Mama."

Jacqueline's grip tightened.

However, I had an opportunity since I have God in my heart to break free from that mindset and do things that seem impossible because I have a supernatural being on my side. But it was hard and challenging—my skin itched, and their belittling remarks felt like barriers I needed to overcome. Still, I hoped to pass through them.

"I just worry, darling. Marriage is more than affection." She continued.

Race controls everything, whether they agreed or not.

It does.

Whether I spoke up about it or not.

It still does.

"It's heritage. Stability. I do wonder how you will raise children who understand where they come from, when they come from… so far away."

I looked at my fiancé while taking a deep breath, and then back to her with parted lips, but no words came out. The silence stretched, thick and arching my soul.

When I walked into their house, that was the first comment she made, and in their minds, they thought, 'Oh, Lord. What is he going to bring to the table?' Because society planted that idea in our minds. I'm sure if Jacqueline came back with a white man, even if he wasn't dressed in the clothes she put me in, they would never have judged or treated him the way they did me.

That I promise you.

"I'm sorry." I apologized for my blackness. "I need a moment."

We work at least two, three jobs and work extra hard all the time to survive.

Even when broken, we have no choice but to bounce back because we've been through life, all the worst and hardest stuff in human nature. And at least, I'm very aware of having grown up in Africa, a place that told me I was enough as a kid, and knowing that around me never changed the way l looked at myself in America.

That I am proudly black and African without seeking anyone else's validation.

And I felt judged; maybe they assumed I didn't know certain things due to my background. And sometimes it weighed me down because I love their daughter, but as I said again, I have God on my side to go through such people who put us in that place.

I walked past the doors into the garden. My shoulders trembled gently, and as I reached the edge of the lawn, I wiped my face with the back of my hand.

Have you ever been second-guessed on what you bring to the table as a black man or generally a man?

Especially in a room full of non-Africans or

African-Americans, my confidence as a man had to convince me that I belonged with her. I can make my fiancé happy. But it was crippling, and amid that situation, I stayed true to myself. It didn't matter anyway. I knew I was worthy of being with her and of stepping into any room. I never regretted coming here to honor my culture, even when her mother didn't like where I came from. Also, Jacqueline followed, barefoot on the stone path. Behind us, her parents processed, sipping their tea, and the click of porcelain against a saucer sounded like a closing door.

"I'll always be happier with you." She whispered into my ear.

CHAPTER TWENTY-EIGHT

The sky over Haidian District turned old, bruised with mottled purple and ash. In a quiet residential area, the air was full of rain scent in concrete and the sterile tang of ethanol. A low haze clung to the streets, lit by the flickering orange of sodium lamps and occasional blue flash of a passing patrol drone. COVID protocols had emptied the city of its usual noise.

No children played around or elders gossiping on stomps.

Just silence, broken by the distant coughs of the neighbors and the soft hums of surveillance. A black government van rolled to a stop outside a modest two-story home tucked behind a row of gingko trees, with yellowish leaves trembling in the wind.

Dr. Mel Ling stepped out first. Her lab coat was replaced by a dark wool overcoat that hung stiffly and loosely over her frame. Her face used to be glassy, but now it was swollen on the left side, with a deep, violent mark blooming beneath her eye. Her lower lip bore the split memory of a recent exchange with Captain Xian and Colonel Wei. Perhaps she had pushed past her job for survival. Also, she pulled an N95 mask off her bruised face.

She seemed overwhelmed by the return to the simple task, and the Americans were on the verge of falling. They misled her when they captured Mr. Liang, crossing the line, and she realized the game was on.

Behind her, four men in black suits fanned out, their earpieces glinting under the porch light. They adjusted their masks and black gloves, their movements precise, and rehearsed; also, their arms carried silenced pistols and wore the insignia of the Ministry, barely visible beneath their coats.

Mel realized her head was on a chopping block tonight, and she scrambled for her life. This had to be her second chance to redeem herself, and she wanted it more than anything in the world.

She badly needed a one-on-one with Dr. Sarah and Colton

A red paper lantern hung limp by the door, leftover from a birthday they must've celebrated the day before. The windows were fogged from the inside, and a baby girl, around two years had drawn a rainbow saying, 'we will survive,' which was tapped to the glass.

"Retrieve the subject, eliminate the witnesses."

She ordered through their earpieces.

Maybe now, the Americans' heads were also at risk, and she was willing to go to hell with them, no matter the heat from the States. Especially Dr. Sarah's push came and shoved her entire reputation. As a woman, she didn't have her back, so Mel had lost trust in her going forward.

Dr. Sarah and Colton were both in civilian clothes as a clean-shaven man entered his house without knocking. Mr. Liang's nose smelled the scent of rice and hand sanitizer. On the coffee table, his eldest daughter's math workbook lay open beside a half-eaten tangerine. And the youngest of his daughter's slippers was pink with cartoon pandas neatly placed by the staircase.

Meilin, their mother, stood in the hallway, her mask pulled down with a pale face.

"They're upstairs," she whispered as the Americans followed him from behind.

The white doctors trusted him more than Mel Ling and felt like she was flipping around, costing the lives of civilians. They would rather get rid of her when they could than watch thousands die.

From the top stairs, Lina peeked down, clutching her rabbit. Su stood beside her, one hand on the banister, and her eyes were wide and uncertain.

Both girls wore cloth masks their mother had sewn, stars and moons on faded cotton. While he ran to hug them, two agents grabbed Dr. Colton and Sarah from behind as they descended, dragging them into the living room. Colton's glasses fell, skittering across the floor. Sarah was shoved against the wall, and her mask was shuffled while they evaluated which one of the two was more valuable. They checked around the place.

"The girls... please, let my wife take the girls!" He hoped these men could reintegrate his family back to their society.

A gunshot cracked the air.

Maybe it wasn't nearly enough.

Mathematically.

Mr. Liang collapsed, his body folded as he struck the edge of the staircase. His mask fluttered to the floor like a fallen petal, and Lina, the youngest of his daughters, ran to her father. These colorless liquids swam in her eye as she screamed, and her tiny fingers reached, pleading.

Did this bearded man feel better?

Another shot and another.

Su ran her hands to her textured lips, sobbing quietly while she dropped down as if her legs had given out. Her unicorn hoodie bunched around her shoulders, and her mask slipped sideways.

The cruelest man had split up the shots on these little angels.

He never once gave them a shot at life.

Nor did he flinch or feel remorse.

What happened to humanity?

He should never have taken those shots…

This pushed Sarah down. She couldn't process what her eyes had witnessed in her mind bank.

Maybe it taught her to hold on, no matter how bad life can become.

For her survival.

Because such moments can break the strongest man down.

Meilin dropped her rounded knees, and as a mother, her fingers trembled as she reached for Su, afraid to touch and confirm what she already knew. Her body was still warm, and fingers curled slightly as if she had been about to gasp her sleeve.

Dr. Sarah struggled with the visuals; her eyes had turned reddish brown, and she sobbed. Also, she knelt beside Lina's body; she was almost a toddler, and these flashes of her son's death preoccupied her.

Mel Ling had stripped away everything from her.

Maybe such times teach us about ourselves.

She had struggled, as most women do, with pregnancy, body image, and death issues of her loved ones. And coming here was really a big challenge, not only with the lithium, but also the loss of lives of these kids. The burden rested on her chest like a Christian cross.

Like any decent human or mother.

The wind rustled the gingko leaves, scattering like forgotten prayers.

"WHY?' Meilin looked up at the agents in extreme agony. "WHY?"

She removed her mask, revealing her emotional bruises.

She wasn't a young woman. "Please forgive me. I have failed as your mother."

Dr. Mel Ling walked inside, close to the window with a rainbow that fluttered in the breeze. Her gloved fingers touched it gently, then turned back to the disarrayed room. One of her agents raised his weapon at Meilin.

"No." Dr. Sarah's voice cracked, maybe from the distress they caused this family, and her bloody arms raised. "I'm sorry for messing around with you."

"Mrs. Humanity… you killed these people, haven't you?"

Mel tightened her jaw with a parched forehead.

And Sarah's fears came forefront. She was willing to go home now.

"Please."

"I wish in my heart. But she has seen more than enough."

Maybe Mel didn't feel anything or care about the bloodshed.

She was a straightforward person; the one she truly cared about was herself. Anyone with common sense could see the malice in her veins. And I believed Mel saw the Ministry as the only team she'd have for the rest of her life, instead of working with and partnering with the Americans.

Meilin crawled to her no longer alive daughters with their hands outstretched.

"Please," Sarah whispered while the whites in her eyes grew larger. "Please."

Trying to soften her walls.

A gunshot parted her forehead while the Americans looked away.

One of the agents grasped Dr. Colton, and he slumped him onto the chair where Meilin used to read. His casual coat was soaked through, his mask discarded. Blood had dried along the collars of his shirt, and his hands trembled on his lap. Across him, Dr. Sarah had kneeled to the floor, wrists zip-tied behind, and her face had swollen from the last blow.

"I'm a survivor." Mel opened up for the first time ever.

"Like Muhammad Ali, I don't go down the street boxing random people."

Sarah wondered whether lying and murdering people was part of her job.

On the coffee table, Mel dropped a certain disk. Silver, and unmarked. Just with a faint fingerprint smudge and unauthorized contained sequences. One of the agents stood beside Colton, arms folded and face unreadable.

"Where did you get it?"

Mel asked Colton as she coughed, blood in her throat.

"He gave it to us. Said it had to be seen before you buried it."

Mel looked up, eyes hollow. "And he trusted you?"

During these times, we questioned who we could trust the most to ensure humanity's survival. Especially as the death toll had doubled. It wasn't about countries anymore, but saving lives.

"He said the world and his daughters deserved better."

Sarah interrupted with a shaking voice. Maybe she considered reestablishing the broken trust because the world needed her.

The silence hit hard while Mel clenched her teeth, and her arms removed the disk, and she slid it into a portable reader. The screen lit up. Sequences scrolled A, O, S, and G with numbers while she leaned in, scanning the data, and her jaws tightened.

"I'm dead." She closed her eyes. "It's late… too late!"

Mel then stared at the staircase where reddish residue had dried in thin, rust-colored lines. "I failed everything."

In life, we get burned at least once, but the problem is that we often don't look past the pain, and sometimes, when we are the ones who caused the burn, we should ask for forgiveness.

CHAPTER TWENTY-NINE

As the choir sang, 'Precious Lord,' the whispers began to rise like steam across the casket, and two lawyers in suits from the Belgian immigration office couldn't help but listen to these two married women of class. 'He was a black man from Africa; all he could provide was another little bondslave.' The dehumanization and the devaluation of our emotions and existence?

Although our backgrounds may look different within our community, no one could ever tell if we're African American or not. I personally wouldn't know! At least before someone opened their mouth, and their accents filled the air. I would instead think we're all a bunch of black flocks who may have a slight difference in shade.

At the end of the day, we're all raising black children, no matter the background or history. We're family, and also operate from the side of love. I have always admired the African Americans' confidence to go out there and chase their dreams in a society that never favors them. I learned to step more into my own voice and speak up for myself.

'Didn't he get locked up once? Drugs or something. He must've had a record.'

The realness and formed irrefutable image of conduct needed to be questioned and held accountable. It was always about race when it came to these people I never met.

They continued, 'She was too good for him. Her mother said so.'

Another voice, older and raspier, "He was never in trouble. In fact, he loved that girl so much."

"How would you've known?"

One of the ladies parched her gypsum-toned forehead.

"I'm their house chef. I saw the way he looked at her."

The redheaded priest, a barrel-chested man with a voice like thunder, proceeded as he stepped back to the pulpit. "We are not here to judge a man by running rumors that chased him."

Life for black flocks is totally different from other groups, even in the definition or measure of success. I would never say anyone experiences what we pass through. It's rough, especially if you don't have a strong backbone or know who you are as a person. We have different set goals, in mind and expectation, because realistically, life tends to be easier when you're close to whiteness.

Jacqueline's shoulders shook, whereas her mother never moved an inch.

"As we stand here to say goodbye to my late fiancé, Ahmed Olaoluwatomijogun, I beg everyone to forgive him on my behalf." Her eyes landed on her mother, and she sobbed so hard. Also, behind her stood a not-young man in a hoodie, head bowed down, and his quivering fingers held a burning cigarette.

"He was so kind. Ahmed followed his heart and taught me what real love is. I never used to love… before I met him."

The congregation became a mosaic of contradictions.

And her anti-blackness became intolerable.

"She was slumming. That's all it ever was."

"The same man who took the cash?"

"How did you know?"

"Her mother told me."

The garden was quiet, except for the soft rustling wind through the lavender and distant whirs of traffic. I stood at the edge of their lawn, shoulders tight, fists buried in my pockets, staring out at the rows of hydrangeas that blurred into a haze of blue and white.

The cuts of her mama's words lingered in my ears like banging drums, casually cruel, and wrapped in her smile, delivered with a compliment every single time she spoke.

Something she said about 'good breeding' and 'knowing my place.' I simply walked out. Jacqueline joined me. I was barefoot on the grass since I had abandoned the loafers she had me in on the stone path. She knew the entire look wasn't me.

"I'm sorry." Her voice was low, but warmed my frail walls.

And she reached for my arm, then paused for consideration. Perhaps she noticed the tightness of my angular jaw with a glint of unshed tears. She stepped closer, her fingers grazing my wrist.

"I'm so sorry," she whispered, and her voice

trembled.

"You! You make me feel different, so loved--she doesn't get to define you. Or us."

"It's never your fault," I spoke.

And the silence between us scratched an inch of my brain, but something tender of our shared defiance grew larger. She leaned her head against my broad shoulder like we could take up the whole world.

"I can never imagine a world without you…. no matter what the universe throws at us."

She grabbed my arm as we stood like two silhouettes against the fading light. The garden, having lots of greens, a bit further from the entrance, held us in a hush. The silence was broken when Jacqueline stared with an infectious smile, defrosting my walls. But above all, she was the lady I loved; it never mattered if anyone ever loved me as long as she did.

Her love was enough for me.

Not only that, but her glassy skin glittered more in the night like a sunflower.

"Where should we go for our honeymoon?"

I grew up in a family where we never had

plenty of choices in life. So I remained stuck, and my mind was in between clouds.

"Anywhere in the world as long as I am with you?"

She continued while her fingers brushed mine.

"Anywhere with you, babe!"

I was reassured as colorless liquid swam in her hazel eyes.

"I appreciate you for being in my life. Choosing me is the greatest gift life has ever given me."

A crunch of heels on gravel broke the spell she may have had on me. Her mother approached us with the same poise she'd worn at the dinner, pearls gleaming and posture impeccable.

However, her expression had changed, less performative, but more calculating. She stopped a few feet away, arms folded, and her eyes scanned me like a ledger.

"I would like a moment alone with him." She said to her daughter, with a more composed tone than usual.

Jacqueline hesitated to leave while her eyes

darted between her mother and me.

But I gave her a small nod and stepped back, lingering out of earshot.

Her mama took a slow breath of death if she never wished to be there while reaching into her purse and pulling out a slim envelope. She held it out shamelessly and handed me like she offered a business card.

"There's a substantial amount in here."

Her brows raised with a cocky grin.

"Enough to start fresh somewhere else. Maybe in Nigeria, or somewhere far from my daughter."

She made me feel so small, as a thirty-three-year-old man, and my textured lips opened without a word. I didn't take it. My gaze remained steady, but unreadable.

*"But why do you **hate** me so much?"*

The type of harm she used wasn't definitive, like getting punched in the face, but instead abstract pain that tends to be a little more under the radar, so she could invalidate my existence without coming off as an owl.

She swallowed. "I'm not saying you're a bad man."

"No amount of money will ever make me not choose HER."

"You must understand… this isn't about love but legacy." She tightened her jaw.

"And you don't want to bet the things I may have to do to protect what we built."

Her body shook as she looked away.

"I worry as her mother---and she has never been good at making choices. Like, who runs so far away in America to work as a waiter when her father is a fucking tycoon?"

One with the right discernment will.

If I had such a mother, I would run away.

And don't take that as an understatement, I loved my mama more than my life, but if she were her, I would've loved and cherished her from a distance. Sometimes, to love takes sacrifice, so you may not know or learn hate from those you look up to.

She had traceable neck muscles with venom. "I'm concerned over my family's reputation, and I am willing to pay you any amount of money."

I glanced at the envelope, then back at her. "You think I'm for sale?"

Was it my coffee skin that made her disrespect me?

Or I lacked integrity and dignity like any other group?"

"I think everyone has a price." She didn't even flinch or reflect like any sensible human. No matter how I hid, my inner emotions got crushed because I badly wanted her to like me. I wished she did. But she instead insulted me with their wealth. And I loved her daughter so much.

I still do.

"I hope you take this opportunity I'm offering you."

The silence became colder than before while I stepped back, letting the envelope fall to the grass untouched. She stared at it and then at me with crisscrossed arms. Also, behind her, Jacqueline watched, fists clenched and heart pounding inside her chest.

CHAPTER THIRTY

The saga of Dr. Sarah versus Mel. And one had to come on top. Whether they came for each other's neck. Or not. The air was thick with the metallic scent of blood. "Wait," Dr. Sarah begged while she stepped forward RIGHT to her face. Against the wall, Dr. Colton sat bound to a chair, and they had already thrown some blows on his way. His casual coat was soaked through at the collar with both sweat and blood. His glasses hung crookedly from his bruised face, one lens shattered.

A gun, black and compact, was aimed at his temple by a stone-faced man in a surgical mask.

On the floor, Dr. Sarah crumpled, her face swollen and streaked with reddish liquid. Her left eye was nearly shut, her lip split, and her breathing shallow. She had tried to crawl toward her workmate earlier, but a swift kick from one of the men had left her ribs fractured.

"We won't say anything about you."

Colton rasped with his cracking voice. However, Mel's alliance with Americans was so unpredictable.

"No one has to know." Dr. Sarah lay still, her hand twitching against the cold floor. "We're not your enemy, Mel. We're here for collaboration." She coughed, a wet, rattling sound.

And she tried to crawl again.

Massive failure on her first try.

Massive failure on her fourth.

Across from her, Dr. Mel Ling's eyes gleamed with something icy cold, and her hands folded behind her. Like she was about to air all their dirty laundry to them.

But she used to tell her late son to get out there and do it. Never rely on anyone for rescue because in life, the only person capable of saving you is yourself. In this situation, Dr. Sarah knew she couldn't rely on her, and she had to do what she had to do to save herself.

Mel stepped back, her polished shoes clocking softly against the bloody floor.

"You were never supposed to see this," the corners of her lips frowned. "And now left me with no choice but…"

"We'll erase everything from the database."

Sarah strengthened herself. "Burn the notes. Please let us go." While these wild voices in her head told her to try again to convince her.

Even when she failed the first attempt. Deep down in her soul, Sarah felt she had the free will and power to change her fate. Because she was there anyway, and had to deal with her roughness.

Mel tilted her head in the process and then nodded in agreement. The Americans exhaled like they had escaped the verge of death. However, there was always a rule in play. You think you have seen enough, double it. Sarah being out there without her son or nagging husband around anymore drained her. However, she used this time to reflect and learn new things about herself.

"Holy moly." The corners of split lips stretched, exposing her teeth stained with reddish residue. "Ah, this next world is truly beautiful." She soliloquized in a not clear tone.

"Wow, I'm so lucky to be here right now."

Sarah soaked the white flashes and took a mental picture and broke from reality because she struggled with her own vision ever since she lost her family, that she even have surgery for her swollen eyes, which may have led to blindness at one time, and at her age.

But now she became thankful to have seen the good and bad of our world. Sarah was emotional. "Wow, I was definitely meant to be here." It felt like she was almost being rewarded for her goodness.

And she was immersed in the beauty and how incredible the universe was in her sight.

"I think I am blessed here, Mel." She raised her metallic tone. "It's just amazing... I feel like the luckiest person right now. Ha-ha---It's funny, I'm laughing and crying at the same time... but I'm the luckiest person."

A shot came fast. Ringing like a thunderclap. Dr. Colton's salt and pepper hair became a bloody birth, and his body jerked then slumped sideways, one arm dangling off the chair, and fingers grazing the floor. His eyes remained open, fixed on the ceiling where baby Su had once taped glow-in-the-dark stars.

Sarah made a sharp, raw wail, but cut short by the second shot. Her body jerked once, then fell still as silence returned, thick and suffocating. Her time was up, and she had already gotten vulnerable. However, when one door closes, the other opens.

"I liked her!" Dr. Mel spat on her, and she turned away, already reaching for her gloves. Her men began clearing the house to make sure the sequence would remain buried. She had jumped like a big shark from the ocean and ate the Americans up.

Jacqueline stood barefoot on their lawn, her heels discarded beside the wrought iron bench. Also, her mama's arms had crossed, standing a few feet away from me as my hands were in my pockets, pulling myself down with jaw clenching and eyes fixed on their doors.

I had hoped to mend the relationship with her mama. It was important in Yoruba culture, so I felt a need to hear her out from day one. I had no idea how I was going to convince her. I aimed to reunite us as a family. But she made it obvious she was coming for me no matter what.

Because her mama sounded like a person used to being in power.

And I knew she was planning to strike fast

and first.

"You're paying him to leave me?" Her voice rang out sharp and stunned.

And her mama turned, startled, composing herself with the icy grace of someone used to controlling others. I grew a desire to know her thoughts and plans while she was in the spotlight.

"I'm protecting you."

She lived her truth as if it weren't that obvious.

But I knew who she was before I even met her.

People used to judge me because of my skin.

And I had to first prove them wrong, *'Oh, he's black. He must be dangerous!"*

This world makes a black man feel lonely.

I had been alone for fifteen years.

Many, many lonely moments.

I had been through a lot in my whole life, and also made an escape goat because of my skin tone. But there was more to me than just the color of my skin. Layers of human, and it hurt being stigmatized as a bad thing in society. We black folks had to look out for each other to be able to survive all the owls' notorious deeds aimed at us.

I stepped forward with a low voice.

"You think I'm dangerous? Or bad influence?"

"I'm only protecting my daughter."

"From what?"

"From this mistake." Her eyes never once flickered. "From a life where you'll always be an outsider."

She was right.

The system never favored dark-skinned people.

And she opposed my partnership with her daughter, who I loved dearly, that I let her cover me in a 4-layer texture of foundation to fit in, and be accepted, also hide my blackness, like I should've felt ashamed.

Or lucky to share a table with them.

However, it was refreshing to have met someone totally different from them. Somebody who is so confident and comfortable in her own skin. She understood me, but Jacqueline came from a family that didn't see me as an equal or even a normal human being.

She had a cracked voice. "You think he's beneath me?"

Thanks to God, she never adapted and pretended to be superior to marginalized groups of people.

And now her mama could see the incredible human she had birthed to the world.

Whether she agreed or not.

She smiled, cold and with no remorse. "I think we all know he's beneath us."

Her mama was my greatest fear because she never once saw me.

The woman did not plan to like me from the get-go.

And it broke my heart, being left out due to my blackness.

But I was a normal human male like Jacqueline's cousin.

It only happened that I had darker skin, and I couldn't even hide behind the 4-layer texture. My fears of losing Jacqueline came forefront, and I became petrified in case she changed her mind and looked at me differently. Or even loved me less.

And not want to be around me anymore.

I feared disappointing her.

Jacqueline's breath caught fire. "You don't get to say things like that or decide for me."

She always supported me against the world.

And had my black back no matter what or who.

We both planned to roll like that.

She narrowed her eyes. "You're young and he's older. He must be manipulating you."

"You don't know me." I tightened my jaw in wonder at what I ever did to deserve such mistreatment. Jacqueline made me realize that sometimes quietness to fit in may overstimulate and mistake me for a weak man. But we black people had to do that to survive, and I remembered how hard that was, especially after the slave trade.

We were stripped of our heritage and given theirs.

Maybe I needed to stand up for myself in this situation.

Her mother picked the envelope. "One hundred thousand euros."

And be *a proud black man* first.

No, I didn't need to blend in.

We were all supposed to meet each other in the middle.

Accept ONE another's cultural background.

Not question mine.

I had to live my truth out there without hiding my blackness.

And funny how much love pushed me to self-loathing for their approval.

"You're disgusting." Her daughter flushed with rage.

"No, I am being real."

I no longer cared how she perceived me.

And I planned to walk out there as a new man.

A different man.

Jacqueline turned to me, her voice trembling but fierce. She operated in a place of hurt. "Let's get married." Her mother pulled her face with disgust. "Tonight. In Brussels."

"Jacqueline..." I blinked, not that I never craved marrying her, but I believed she may not have been in the right state of mind. The truth I would trade my life for being her husband in this lifetime and another.

I appreciated her for being in my life.

"I'm serious. I want to be your wife tonight."

It felt like a huge weight had been lifted from my shoulders.

And I would take her to be my wife for the rest of my life.

And forever.

Her mama's voice rose, and lines parched her forehead.

"You're not leaving this house, young lady."

But she had already moved, grabbing my hand, and we ran, wild and free, through their garden. Her joyful laughter sharpened, exposing her pretty dimples, and behind us, her mama's voice sliced through the night as we ran past the hedges, down the gravel path leading to their side gate.

I was excited and ready for the next phase of our lives.

Because I loved her.

And still do.

'Faster!" Jacqueline gasped, and I couldn't help but smile. She managed to bring out the young side of me. Filling me with some youthful flames I lost after the death of my mama, and I couldn't remember when I last smiled like that.

"You're insane." My voice was low and incredulous.

"I'm in love with you," she shot back, and I brushed our soulful eyes, gleaming.

She made me believe in love again. I mean, I last dated fifteen years ago.

Chioma and I were friends at secondary school for a year, and I may have taken things a little further, but maybe we were only friends. Eventually, we started dating, but very slowly, and like, we both saved ourselves for marriage.

But is fifteen years a long time?

And yes, *I was a virgin thirty-three-year-old man.*

Her parents' mansion erupted behind us while her mama shouted, the butler and their chef chased us, and the driver scrambled to start the car. We were like teenagers sneaking out barefoot and sticking together.

We burst onto Rue du College, breathless, wild, and laughing through the tears. Such little gestures made life worth a pursuit, and I couldn't tell when I last let loose. Also,

Brussels shimmered around us, lamplight on the cobblestones, and the scent of rain and rebellion.

We were bound to love one another.

"You sure about this?" I paused while my chest became heavy. No lady had ever done something crazy for me. Honestly, it felt alive to run with the love of my life.

She turned, her brunette hair tousled, and her cheeks flushed.

"I'm sure about you."

A cab rolled past, and she flagged it down with a dramatic wave. The driver with a beard blinked at her and my torn shirt, at the chaos trailing behind us. He opened the door and we hailed a cab, ducking low as it sped toward the city center.

She clutched my hand while we were away from her family.

"She'll never forgive me."

I looked at her as she shook slightly.

Like she was about to cry.

Sometimes we have to let go of our past for the love and happiness we craved. And in such moments in life, we either fold and be stranded in such a sick cycle of hatred or prevail and progress with a perceptive beyond tomorrow's expectations.

"I'll always be here for you."

I understood the weight and price it took as I kissed her soft temple.

Bad people make us second-guess our choices even when it's the right thing to do.

I believe we should all be flexible and open to knowing others solely through love. Drawing these impossible lines only caused harm and division in our society, rather than progress. Growing up is realizing we're all equal regardless of our skin color.

She grinned. "Let's be scandalous."

Each word came sporadically from my lips; I never saw a world without her, no matter how easy or difficult our marriage may turn. We passed shuttered cafes and glowing cathedrals as Jacqueline pulled out her phone, searching for a civil registrar open late.

And I watched her in wonder, impressed. "You really want to become my wife tonight?"

The whites in her hazel eyes grew large. "I want to be your woman forever."

Her fingers traced the line of my jaw, and we leaned close, eating each other's lips and our eyes shut. She made me feel all these dreamy emotions. "You're beautiful!"

Also brought the best version of myself. I was confident and at the same time fearful. Growing up in Nigeria, I used to be a scared boy, following my background, and when I moved to a new country, I gained some 'independence,' accepting parts of myself I never used to cherish or even realized I had.

The black magic!

My blackness became real.

And visual to the eye.

I had to learn how to survive, including the times I shouldn't be out there.

Because my life would be at risk.

Or only touching a single product at a time in a store.

Because there wouldn't be a second chance in case.

Paranoia or fear befell the seller.

Oh, and also no room for letting them see you sweat.

We arrived at a modest municipal building

tucked between two galleries and the high vaulted ceiling of a late-night civil office, with a sleepy clerk and a bouquet we bought from the street vendor.

There are times when we do everything we suppose, and now have to trust our inner human. My younger and African self would not have been able to process the situation, but my older self, I've had some life experience to realize what's right or wrong, and I didn't feel any nauseous emotion inside my frail walls when I looked at my heart.

I loved her and she loved me.

She slammed her ID on the counter. "We're getting married. Now."

The bald clerk blinked. "Do you have any witnesses?"

She turned toward me. "Do we need them?"

I shrugged. "We have each other."

That's all we ever needed. Anyway.

To rely on one another.

And the bond we built.

Though there was a part of me that felt bad for Jacqueline.

Because my existence may have destroyed

the relationship she shared with her parents.

Or even the chances of ever returning home.

Our ceremony was brief.

No guests or Champagne.

Just two signatures, two trembling hands, and a kiss that tasted like flames.

She leaned against me while her heart raced like banging drums. "We did it."

My mama must've been super proud of me. She had to be, and I kept on seeing my funeral throughout my mind, yet the universe had other plans for my wife and me. It was always about my person. The lady I meant to be with all the span of time, no matter the gunning from unhappy people.

And yes, I worried.

All the time.

Because I want her and our future children to know me for who I am.

Not my skin complexion.

All the good qualities about me.

I wrapped my broad arms around her. "We did."

She looked up at me, mischievous, and these steamy series flashed through my mind.

"Now what?"

I smiled. "Now we live."

www.ingramcontent.com/pod-product-compliance
Lightning Source LLC
Chambersburg PA
CBHW061625250726
48659CB00004B/1088